FOCUS ON THE FAMILY®

SIERRA JENSEN SERIES

P9-ELV-157

Hold On Tight

ROBIN JONES GUNN

BETHANY HOUSE PUBLISHERS
MINNEAPOLIS, MINNESOTA 55438

A Focus on the Family book published by
Bethany House Publishers
A Ministry of Bethany Fellowship International
11300 Hampshire Avenue South, Minneapolis, Minnesota 55438
www.bethanyhouse.com

Printed in the United States of America by
Bethany Press International, Minneapolis, Minnesota 55438

Library of Congress Cataloging-in-Publication Data
Gunn, Robin Jones, 1955–
   Hold on tight / Robin Jones Gunn.
     p. cm. — (The Sierra Jensen series ; 10)
   Summary: While on a trip to Southern California with her friends and
her brother, who is scouting out potential colleges, Sierra realizes that she
must soon make some decisions about her life.
   ISBN 1–56179–637–9
   [1. Voyages and travels—Fiction. 2. California, Southern—Fiction.
3. Christian life—Fiction.] I. Title. II. Series: Gunn, Robin Jones, 1955–
Sierra Jensen series ; 10.
PZ7.G972Ho   1998
[Fic]—dc21   98–21106
                                         CIP
                                         AC

98 99 00 01 02 03 04 05 / 15 14 13 12 11 10 9 8 7 6 5 4 3 2 1

To Cindy and Carrie,

with a grateful heart,

for all the Tuesday mornings

we've spent together.

chapter one

*S*IERRA JENSEN STEPPED INSIDE MAMA BEAR'S BAKERY. She had worked here for almost a year but never tired of the fresh fragrance of cinnamon and warm bread that greeted her as the tiny bell over the door announced her entrance. This clear spring afternoon she wasn't working. She was meeting friends.

Glancing at the empty corner table by the front window, Sierra realized she was the first one to arrive for the Monday afternoon gathering. For months she and her friends Vicki and Amy had bent their heads close together over that same table every Monday at 4:00. They shared secrets, settled arguments, gave free advice, and teased each other mercilessly.

Mrs. Kraus, the owner of Mama Bear's, called to Sierra from behind the counter. "I just pulled out a pan of fresh rolls. Will you girls be sharing your usual large, warmed-up one with an extra dab of frosting?"

"I'm sure we will," Sierra said. Six other customers were seated in the bakery, and Mrs. Kraus appeared to be the only person working in the front of the shop. "Would you like me to get the tea for us?"

"No, I think I can remember what you always have. I'll get it." The cheerful, round Mrs. Kraus turned to greet an older woman who had entered the shop.

Sierra settled her slim frame into her usual chair, welcoming the stream of sunshine that spilled through the window and cascaded down her long, blonde curls. She loved the feelings of promise this time of year brought, especially this spring. It was her senior year in high school, and endless possibilities stretched out for her future. That was probably why she felt impatient for Amy and Vicki to show up. She had a very promising possibility to tell them about.

Across the street a battered old Volvo pulled into a metered parking space. Sierra watched as petite Amy flipped her sunglasses onto the top of her head and fingered the ends of her short, dark hair at the base of her neck. Amy glanced right and left and then hurried across the street. Her dash had a slight zigzag pattern to it. She kept her head down and didn't watch where she was going.

That's the way Amy approaches life, Sierra thought, *zigzagging with her head down. I'll have to tell her that.*

"Personality observations" is what Vicki had first labeled these insights, when she communicated to Sierra that the way Sierra bit her lower lip was a sign of worry. Sierra accepted the observation with grateful surprise. She had never realized she bit her lower lip.

Amy, however, wasn't interested in observations lately. The openness she had demonstrated in February was gone by the beginning of March, and it didn't seem to be returning. Sierra was just glad that, even though Amy hadn't been saying much during their get-togethers, at least she kept coming. Sierra had nearly lost her friendship with Amy once, and she didn't want that to happen again.

When Amy entered, Sierra smiled and waved. The pair had certainly experienced their ups and downs in their year of friendship. In spite of their differences, they respected and deeply cared for each other, and that's what kept them close.

"Vicki's not here yet?" Amy said, slipping into a chair across from Sierra.

Sierra shook her head. "When I saw her at lunch, I told her I had something to tell you guys, so I thought she would be the first one here."

"Guess you'll have to tell me first, then," Amy said, her dark eyes glancing at Sierra's outfit. "I like that shirt. When did you get it?"

"Believe it or not, I found it stuffed in a bag Mom was taking to the Salvation Army. I think it was Tawni's. I'm actually wearing something my sister liked!"

Amy reached over and felt the sleeve of Sierra's lavender chenille top. "I like this material. It sure brings out the blue in your eyes." Amy smiled as she added, "If you get tired of it, you can always toss it in my direction."

Mrs. Kraus arrived at their table, balancing a tray with their snack. Sierra reached for the mugs of hot tea, and Amy grabbed the plate with the cinnamon roll.

"It's my turn to pay," Amy said. "I'll bring it up to the register, Mrs. Kraus."

"No hurry. Just enjoy," Mrs. Kraus said.

The bell above the door announced Vicki's arrival. She swished past Mrs. Kraus and, with a flushed face, began to talk before she even sat down. "Sorry! I was almost out of gas, and I didn't have any money, so I had to go to the bank, and the line at the drive-up was terrible and, oh, you already ordered? I wanted iced tea today. I think I'll get myself a glass of ice and turn this into iced tea. Anyone else want anything?"

Both Sierra and Amy shook their heads.

Vicki swept past the tables to the counter. Watching her,

Sierra thought about the contrast between her two friends. If Amy zigzagged through life with her head down, Vicki moved through her days at full speed, with her chin to the sky and the wind in her long, silky, brown hair. That zestful optimism eventually had linked Sierra and Vicki, even though Sierra originally had interpreted Vicki's bold approach to life as conceit. Of course, when they first met, Vicki did have an overly active bent toward flirting and was far more interested in developing relationships with guys than with girls.

Amy pulled off a corner of the cinnamon roll. "Do you suppose we can start eating without Vicki? I'm starved."

"Sure. She'll be right back." Sierra pulled her peppermint tea bag out of the mug. With a glance at Vicki, she wondered how her friends would describe her approach to life. Did they see her as a zigzagger or as someone with her face to the sun? She felt she had changed a lot during the past year, and she knew that Vicki and Amy had changed, too. What would they be like a year from now? Or even six months from now, when they all would begin their freshman year of college?

The instant Vicki returned to their table, Sierra spilled her news. "Okay, are you both ready for my big announcement?"

"It can't be that huge if you didn't tell me at lunch today and made me wait until now," Vicki said, carefully pouring her steaming tea over the glass of crushed ice.

"I wanted to tell you both at the same time."

"I appreciate that," Amy said. Amy had changed schools this year after her parents' divorce. She was at a public high school now, instead of at Royal Academy, the small, private Christian school where the three originally had met.

"So?" Vicki prompted.

"Last night my brother called and told me he's going to

Southern California next week. He's pretty sure he wants to attend Rancho Corona University for his master's degree, but he wanted to check out the school before he made a final decision."

"That's your big news?" Vicki asked. Her pretty face took on a teasing grin. "You definitely could have told me that at lunch."

"Wait," Sierra said, her enthusiasm unruffled. "He's going to drive down there next week, and he asked if I wanted to go with him, and my parents said yes!"

"Good for you," Vicki said. "Bring back a surfer for each of us."

"Didn't you go to California last year for Easter vacation?" Amy asked.

"Yes."

"And you also flew down there for your friends' wedding last summer." Amy turned her lower lip into a friendly pout. "How do you expect us to be happy for you again? You keep going on these adventures, and we don't go anywhere. I've never been to California—ever—in my life. I've only been to Seattle—once."

"I hope you have a good time," Vicki said cheerfully to Sierra.

Sierra broke into a wide grin. "You mean you hope *we* have a good time."

" 'We' meaning you and Wes?" Vicki ventured. "Or 'we' meaning the three of us?"

"All of us!" Sierra spouted. "My brother is driving my parents' van down, and they said I could invite my friends to go. We should be able to get an excused absence from school, since it's a college scouting trip. Wes said he would let us check out as many different campuses as we want, as long as he can spend a day at Rancho Corona."

"I'm in," Vicki said without a moment's hesitation.

"What kind of colleges?" Amy asked cautiously.

"Amy!" Vicki nudged her arm. "You just said you never get to go anywhere. Accept the invitation and say thank you."

Amy hesitated a moment before saying, "It *would* be kind of fun."

"When do we leave?" Vicki asked.

"Wednesday after school," Sierra said. "I'm going to drive the van down to Corvallis, and then Wes and I will take turns driving from there. It's going to take us at least 20 hours, so we'll sleep in the van. In Los Angeles, we'll stay with a couple Wesley knows."

"Where is Rancho Corona University?" Vicki asked.

"I don't know. Someplace down there. It's about an hour's drive from where my sister lives, so we might stay with her the next night."

"This is going to be so much fun!" Vicki sipped her iced tea and glanced at Amy for a sign of enthusiasm.

"When do we come back?" Amy asked.

"Late Sunday night. It'll be a really packed couple of days, but I think it's going be great. You do want to come, don't you?"

Amy nodded, but she still didn't look overly excited. "I'll have to get off work and clear everything with my mom."

"Me, too," Vicki said. "But that shouldn't be a problem."

"Thanks for reminding me," Sierra said. "I forgot I have to ask Mrs. Kraus for the days off."

"She always lets you adjust your schedule," Vicki said. "I'm sure she'll be her sweet self and give you the time off. Now let's just pray my boss is as understanding."

Sierra laughed. "Your boss? Why wouldn't he be?"

Vicki's boss was her dad. Mr. Navarone owned a large car dealership in Portland, and Vicki worked there part-time doing clerical work.

"I know," Vicki said. "He'll let me off. My dad is going to be thrilled I'm showing serious interest in going to college. He'll probably not only send me off with his blessing but also with enough spending money to treat everyone to a trip to an amusement park down there."

Amy's expression lit up. "Could we go do that? Really? How about Universal Studios? Do you guys think we could squeeze in a trip to Universal Studios? Or at least to Hollywood?"

"I don't see why not," Sierra answered. "Wes said we could plan whatever we wanted."

The three friends bent their heads close. As the spring sunshine lit their little corner of the world, they pulled apart their cinnamon roll and began to make plans for their upcoming road trip. Sierra felt a gleeful rush of anticipation and knew the next week and a half couldn't speed by fast enough for her.

chapter two

"AMY AND VICKI ARE BOTH COMING," SIERRA SAID to her brother that night on the phone. "Hope you don't mind carting the three of us around."

"No," Wes said calmly. He had inherited many of their father's characteristics, including a willingness to take on challenges with a shrug of the shoulders. "I think four is a good number. We'll have room to sleep in the van, and it won't be too much to ask of my friends when we stay at their house. You told the girls we're driving straight through, didn't you?"

"Yes."

"And that we're spending a day at Rancho Corona?"

"Yes. Where is that college, anyway?"

"It's near Temecula. South of Lake Elsinore."

Those coordinates meant nothing to Sierra.

"Don't you remember my telling you about it? I'm sure they have a Web site, if you want to check it out before we go down. It might be a good idea to look up all the colleges you want to visit ahead of time on the Internet and contact them to see if they have any restrictions or requirements for touring their campuses."

"Good idea. Vicki, Amy, and I came up with three colleges we would like to visit, and then Rancho Corona, of course. Oh, and Wes? How do you feel about including something fun on the trip?"

"Something fun? I thought spending five days with me would be about as much fun as any girl could ask for."

"Very funny. I mean like going to Universal Studios or something."

"Fine with me. Make sure you have enough money. None of those places is cheap."

"Do you have a preference of where we go?" Sierra asked.

"Since you're asking, I'd say Magic Mountain. I'm more interested in roller coasters than movie stars. But I'll leave it up to you and your friends."

After Sierra hung up, she sat on the living room couch for a long while, thinking. She could hear her mom in the kitchen, unloading the dishwasher. From upstairs her dad was telling her two little brothers to climb into bed. Granna Mae was quietly tucked in her comfortable, large bedroom. Sierra could sit alone with her thoughts.

The first thought was about Amy and Wes. Last summer Amy had made it clear she had a huge crush on Sierra's brother. Wesley had never given Amy reason to think he was interested in her, at least from anything Sierra had ever noticed. Now Amy hadn't seen Wesley for months, since he had gone back to school in the fall at Oregon State University in Corvallis. Sierra had no way of knowing until they met up in Corvallis next week if Amy would show an interest in Wes again. The potential Amy-Wes relationship made Sierra nervous.

Then there was the choice of what fun outing they should include. Amy seemed pretty set on Universal Studios, but since Wes was their host, Sierra thought he should choose the amusement park. Vicki wouldn't care which one they went to. Neither did Sierra. Once again, it was a thing between Amy and Wes.

Sierra bit her lower lip and then realized she was doing it and stopped. *This is crazy. I'm getting in a froth over nothing. I'll call Amy and tell her Wes suggested we go to Magic Mountain. She'll understand since it was Wes's choice. But wait. If she gives in to Wes's choice, does that mean she's trying to score points with him? Should I just come right out and ask her if she's still interested in him? Maybe I should ask Vicki what she thinks I should do. No, that would be talking about Amy behind her back. If I'm going to talk to anybody, it should be Amy.*

Sierra decided she would talk to Amy. But not tonight. Instead, she would wait another day and hope the queasy feelings about Wes and Amy would go away. Why did that bother her so much anyway?

Getting up from the couch, Sierra went into the kitchen and opened the refrigerator in search of brain food.

"How's the homework coming along?" her mom asked.

"I was just going to start it," Sierra answered. She didn't turn around, but she could almost feel her mother looking at the clock, noticing it was after 8:30, and looking back at Sierra with mild concern that it was so late and she hadn't even started her homework. For the past two months, Sierra had burned the midnight oil over the excessive amount of homework she had. Whoever had told her it got easier at the end of her senior year had definitely gone to some school other than Royal Academy. Between work, volunteering at the Highland House, church activities, and her mound of schoolwork, Sierra barely had a social life. That was probably why she was so excited about the California getaway.

"I know," Sierra said without turning to catch her mother's gaze. "I should have started sooner. But don't worry. I actually don't have too much tonight. Besides, I had to call Wesley and talk to him about the trip. Do we have any orange juice?"

"In the freezer," her mom said. "What about Mama Bear's? Were you able to get the time off?"

"Yes," Sierra said, opening the freezer and pulling out a can of frozen orange juice. "Mrs. Kraus told me it was no problem, but I have to work this Friday after school." She reached in the cupboard for a pitcher and went to work making up the orange juice.

Mrs. Jensen closed the door of the dishwasher and wiped off the counter. "Good," she said. "I think this is going to be a helpful trip for both you and Wesley. Do you think you would like to apply to Rancho Corona? I'm wondering if we should start filling out some of the paperwork before you go down."

"Dad said to wait, since the application fee is kind of high and he's already put out the money for those other three applications last fall."

Sierra had managed to keep a 4.0 grade average since junior high, although it didn't seem like a big deal to her. The way she saw it, she simply had a mind that easily collected necessary information, spilled it back on a test a few days later, and then promptly forgot anything that didn't hold a special attraction for her. She didn't see herself as smart; she merely knew how to work the system. That was to her advantage, since she already had received two scholarship offers and had been accepted at the three colleges she had applied to last fall. At this point, it was pretty much up to her to decide which college she went to, since her parents had been in favor of all her choices.

Well, almost all. There was one they'd said no to. The University of Edinburgh.

"Was there any mail for me today?" Sierra asked.

"I don't think so. Did you check the chair in the study?"

Sierra had a favorite chair in the room that her dad used as his office. It had once been the library of this large Victorian house that Sierra's great-grandfather had built in 1915. Since last fall Sierra had been involved in a lively correspondence with Paul MacKenzie, a tenderhearted guy she had met more than a year ago at Heathrow Airport in England. Her parents had gotten into the habit of putting his letters on Sierra's favorite chair in the study. They knew that's where she would go to read them.

The emotional involvement Sierra felt with Paul through his letters had reached an all-time high for her last December. But when she realized she was far more into their correspondence than he appeared to be, she had backed off. Instead of writing him nearly every day, she began to write him about once every two weeks, which was the same pace he had been writing to her all along.

During January, Paul had written only twice—one short letter and one even shorter postcard. His words were always rich with sincerity, never flirty or demanding. Paul openly visited with her through his letters without hinting at anything strongly emotional on his side. He never signed his letters with the word "love." Yet to Sierra, the kind, earnest, from-the-heart friendship he had expressed was far closer to the best kind of love there was. She believed in many ways it was stronger than anything she or her girlfriends shared with any of the guys they liked.

That quiet hope kept Sierra writing to Paul. In February she had sent him a valentine. She made it from a collage of pictures and words she had cut from magazines and glued to a red heart. It said, " 'God is love. . . . We love because he first loved us' (1 John 4:16, 19)." The verse seemed an appropriate way to communicate that, yes, this was a valentine; but, no, it wasn't about Sierra revealing her love for Paul or her desire for a deeper relationship with him. It was about God and His never-ending love for both of them.

That's truly where Sierra had stored away her friendship with Paul. It was hidden in the shelter of God's love for those who abide in Him. However, Sierra had discovered she still felt warm emotions when she held one of Paul's letters in her hand.

Pouring herself a glass of orange juice and returning the pitcher to the fridge, Sierra slipped out of the kitchen and checked her favorite chair. No letters awaited her.

"That's okay," she whispered in the quiet room that smelled of old books. "You just take good care of him, will You, God? I know You've been working in huge ways in Paul's life lately, and I'm really thankful. I guess I just want to ask that You protect him and keep him safe at his school in Edinburgh. Help him decide what to do about school next year. I know he has to make that decision in the next few weeks, and it's been really hard for him. Thanks, Lord."

Sierra turned on the computer at her dad's desk. Before she started her homework, she wanted to check out the Web site for Rancho Corona, as Wesley had suggested. As she typed in the search information, Sierra thought of how she had never tried to locate information about the university Paul attended in Scotland. Last fall she had announced to her parents, without having any information, that that was where she wanted to start her freshman year of college. All she knew was that Paul went there. Her parents said no, and she never had searched out any details about enrolling.

Tonight Sierra felt a struggle. She knew she should be content with this college scouting trip Wesley was taking her on, and she should be willing to select one of the colleges at which she had already been accepted, but something inside her refused to let go of Scotland. It was as if a closet door in her heart was pushing its way open. She thought that door had been tightly locked up months ago, after she had swept away the dreams of attending the same college as Paul. But tonight the door of that forgotten closet seemed to open a sliver. The dim light that peeked from the opening beckoned to her.

Instead of typing in "Rancho Corona University," Sierra found her fingers typing "University of Edinburgh, Scotland."

chapter three

"WHAT DO YOU MEAN RANDY SAID YES?" SIERRA stared at Vicki in the school parking lot. The bell was about to ring, and if they didn't move, they would both be late for their first-period class.

"I called Randy last night and told him about the trip, and he said yes, he wants to come with us. He's going to ask the other guys in the band to see if they want to come, too. I told them we have free places to sleep, but they have to bring enough money for their own food."

Sierra continued to stare at Vicki. The bell rang, but she didn't move.

"Sierra, we're late! Come on. We can go through all the details at lunch." Vicki started toward the building.

"I never said anything about inviting anyone else, Vicki!" Sierra hurried after her friend. "Why did you ask him?" Sierra thought she knew the answer. For months Vicki had been interested in Randy even though he treated Vicki, Sierra, and all girls the same. Vicki must have thought a few days in a van with Randy as a captured audience might help her win his affections.

"There's plenty of room in your van. Your parents adore Randy. He and Wes get along great. What's the problem?"

"Well . . . it's you, Vicki."

"Me?" Vicki stopped at the front door of the school. The innocent expression on her face maddened Sierra.

"Never mind," Sierra said, holding up a hand in defeat and turning away from her friend. "I'll see you at lunch." As Sierra went through the door, she was still boiling inside.

She dashed to her class and was thankful when her teacher waved her to her seat, meaning Sierra didn't have to go to the office for a tardy slip. It was one of the rewards for being an "A" student and rarely coming to class late. Some students were late so regularly they had developed a routine of stepping to the back of the class, pausing, getting a nod from the teacher, and then going to the office for their most recent tardy slip.

But it barely mattered to Sierra that she had been waved to her seat. Her mind at that moment was anywhere but in the classroom. What was her brother going to say? Or her parents? How could she uninvite Randy after Vicki had invited him? Fortunately, Randy was a close enough buddy that she thought he would understand if she explained the situation to him. But why should she have to? It would be fun to have Randy along, too—as long as the rest of the band didn't come. Warner, the drummer, drove Sierra crazy. If he came, the whole trip would be ruined for her.

Why am I even thinking this? This is my trip. For my friends. At my invitation. I can say yes or no to whomever I want.

By lunch Sierra had prepared her line of defense. She would say her parents and brother would decide who could go and who couldn't. If they thought Randy should come along, then he could come. Neither her parents nor her brother would think Warner should come along because

Sierra would tell them it wasn't a good idea. That would take the pressure off her.

When Sierra entered the cafeteria, her usual bunch of lunchtime friends were gathered around "their" table. They all looked up at her and started to talk before she sat down.

"Hey, Sierra," Tre, one of the guys in the band, said, "Vicki told us we have to pay for our food and that's all. Don't you want us to pay something for the gas, too?"

"Are you guys going to the beach?" Margo, one of the girls at the table, asked. "If you are, I'm definitely going."

"I checked at the office," Randy said. "We do get an excused absence, since the trip is to visit colleges."

"Cool. Count me in," said Margo.

Vicki still wore her innocent expression when Sierra, standing her ground, shot Vicki a perturbed look and said, "You guys have to understand something. It's not up to me. My brother is the one heading up this trip, and he and my parents will decide who can go. I didn't mean for it to become an open invitation."

"How many can fit in your van?" Warner asked.

Sierra clenched her teeth. "Eight. But that's beside the point."

Warner did a quick count. "Only four of us want to go."

Vicki held out her fingers and kept counting. "Then Sierra, Amy, Wes, and me. Eight. That's perfect."

Sierra gave Vicki her most exasperated look. "It's not up to me. Didn't you hear what I just said? I'll have to ask my parents and brother."

"Can you let us know tomorrow?" Margo asked. "Vicki said you were planning to visit the college where my parents met. I know they would let me go to see their alma mater."

Sierra found it hard to stay irritated with Margo, who had

no idea this wasn't a free-for-all. Actually, Sierra realized she wouldn't mind if Margo came along. While it hadn't occurred to Sierra to invite her, it would be nice if Margo did come. She had arrived at Royal Academy this year, fresh from the mission field. Her parents had served for years in Peru. Margo slowly had blossomed into a fun friend who was always doing little things for their group, such as bringing cookies to share or sticking notes of encouragement in their lockers. Sierra would feel bad not returning some kindness to Margo now that the opportunity was before her.

"I'll try to let you know tomorrow," Sierra promised. This was becoming complicated. How could she tell her friends that Wes had said yes to Randy, Tre, and Margo but no to Warner? Especially when everyone knew the van had enough seats. That in itself might be the deciding factor, since Wesley had said he thought four people was a good number. There would be very little sleeping if everyone had to sit up the whole way.

I guess the easiest, fairest answer would be to tell everyone, "Sorry, but you can't come." Everyone except Vicki and Amy. And maybe Randy. Oh, and Margo. Man, this is turning into a nightmare!

Sierra wanted to express her frustration to Vicki but forced herself to bite her tongue and wait so she wouldn't say anything she would regret later. Plenty of times in her life she had exploded first, then thought about what she had said later. Those times always required an apology on her part, and she wasn't interested in starting off this trip with hurt feelings all around.

By the time she had explained the situation to her parents after dinner, her dad had a strained look on his face. The skin on his forehead had turned into a bunch of ripples and

tightened between his eyebrows. It looked as though a headache was starting from the outside and working its way to
the inside. Sierra knew exactly how that felt.

"Well," her mom said, breathing a deep sigh, "let's think
this through."

"Only you, Sierra," her dad said, shaking his head.

All Sierra's defenses rose to the surface. "Hey, I didn't
mean for this to happen. Vicki shouldn't have said anything
without asking me first."

"Did you tell her that?" her mom asked.

"No. I knew if I tried to say something, it wouldn't come
out very nice."

"Good for you on that account," her mom said. She
reached across the dining room table and gave Sierra's hand
a squeeze. "We know you didn't try to complicate things, so
don't think you're being blamed for anything."

"All I meant," her dad said, "was that only you would find
yourself caught in such a situation. You tend to end up in
these tangles. I do understand it wasn't your intention, and
we can work this out. Let's give Wesley a call to see what he
thinks."

They tried to call Wes until 11:00 that night but only got
his voice mail. After leaving four messages, Mr. Jensen suggested they go to bed and call Wes in the morning before
Sierra left for school.

"Just tell your friends tomorrow that you don't have an
answer yet. They can wait one more day," Mrs. Jensen said
diplomatically.

Right, Sierra thought. *You try showing up at school tomorrow without an answer and see how popular you are, Mom.*

Sierra went to her bedroom and closed the door. It bugged
her that her room was such a mess. Usually, she could go

weeks without noticing the clutter, but when one area of her
life was unsettled, all the unorganized parts seemed intensi-
fied. She didn't have the desire or energy to clean her room,
since it was so late. It actually made her miss Tawni, her neat-
freak sister, who, when they shared the room, used to insist
Sierra periodically plow through her stuff scattered all over
the place. Ever since Tawni had moved out, Sierra, for the
first time in her life, had dictated her own living conditions.
Only once or twice had her room ever been completely
cleaned since then, and that was when company was antici-
pated.

Reaching for the printed-out information she had gathered from the Internet the night before, Sierra flopped onto
her bed and read again about the University of Edinburgh.
She had a map of the campus and a guide to each of the
buildings. It was morning now in Scotland. Was Paul on his
way to class? Which building would he be in? The James
Clerk Maxwell Building? Or maybe the Ogston Building. She
noticed a spot marked Student Centre. It made her wonder
whom he spent his lunch hours with. Was he ever tardy to
class because of goofy friends who complicated his life by
making plans that didn't coordinate with his?

Sierra put down the papers. It was useless to slip into a
daydreaming mode about Paul. She had done that before,
and it had only produced a deep, insatiable longing. She
didn't want to visit that place again. In her heart of hearts,
she knew she wanted her love to be focused on God, the only
One who could fill her completely. She didn't want to live on
that raw emotional edge where fantasy and imagination
devoured reality.

With a heavy sigh, Sierra reached for her Bible on her
nightstand and pulled out a note card on which she had

written 2 Corinthians 10:3–5 from a different version. She had been trying to memorize the passage, but for some reason it wouldn't stay in her mind. A guest speaker for their youth group had challenged all of them to memorize these verses to learn how to control their imaginations.

She read them aloud in the lonely, cluttered room: " 'For though we walk in the flesh, we do not war after the flesh: (For the weapons of our warfare are not carnal, but mighty through God to the pulling down of strong holds;) Casting down imaginations, and every high thing that exalteth itself against the knowledge of God, and bringing into captivity every thought to the obedience of Christ" (KJV).

" '. . . bringing into captivity every thought to the obedience of Christ,' " she repeated, trying to get the last section to stay in her memory.

Pulling herself up to change into her pajamas and to brush her teeth, Sierra silently prayed. She had plenty to pray about: this mess with her friends and the road trip; her thoughts and imagination wanting to go wild over Paul; and her choice of a college. Now that she had information on Edinburgh, it was even harder not to imagine what it would be like to go there. Her motive was to be near Paul, and certainly that couldn't be an appropriate objective, could it?

Sierra had a hard time sleeping with so many thoughts rushing over her. For some reason she remembered Wesley's words from the night before when he said he preferred roller coasters. Right now, her stomach felt as though she were on one. It looked as if it was going to be an emotional ride that wasn't going to stop anytime soon.

Sierra took hold of her blankets, pulled them up to her chin, and closed her eyes tight. Sleep finally found her.

chapter four

W HEN SIERRA STOOD BEFORE HER FRIENDS AT LUNCH the next day, she felt her heart racing. She told them she hadn't talked to Wes yet, so she didn't have a decision for them.

"I can't get off work anyway," Tre said. "You can take me off the list."

"I know someone else who wanted to go," Margo said.

"Who?" Vicki asked.

"Drake. Maybe he could take your place, Tre, if you're not going."

Sierra's heart raced even faster. Drake, the school's best athlete and biggest flirt, had been interested in Sierra last summer, and she had returned the interest. They even went out—sort of. It was never a defined dating relationship, but it certainly was a relationship that had caused Sierra confused feelings and lots of conflicts with her friends—especially Amy. Amy had been interested in Drake before he asked Sierra to go out with him.

Even though Sierra and Drake were still casual friends, they rarely spoke to each other. She could only imagine what it would be like to be in a van for days with Amy and Drake, not to mention everyone else. Her head was beginning to pound in time to her heart. She couldn't stand this much longer.

"You guys," Sierra stated with a rush of adrenaline, "you need to know this trip wasn't supposed to be an open invitation. It's turning into a huge mess. I didn't know Vicki was going to ask you all to come. If I'd known, I would have told her not to invite you." The words tumbled out before she had a chance to evaluate them.

"Are you saying you don't want any of us to go?" Margo asked.

"You never said anything about its being a closed trip," Vicki blurted out. "All you said was Wes agreed to drive you and some of your friends. I thought there was room for all our friends. Why didn't you tell me it was supposed to be just you, Amy, and me?"

"I thought you understood that."

"Obviously not," Vicki said, folding her arms.

"We don't have to go," Randy said quickly, trying to bring peace to a situation full of rising tension. "It's no big deal. We understand, Sierra. It's your trip. We all kind of took over and didn't let you invite the ones you wanted."

Now Sierra felt bad. "Randy, it wasn't that I was trying to invite only certain people . . ."

"But that's what you did," Warner said. "The ones you invited were Amy and Vicki."

"That was her choice," Margo said. "She can invite whomever she wants. You guys are trying to make her feel bad."

"No we're not," Warner said.

"I can't go anyway," Tre said, shrugging his shoulders. He left the table to return his cafeteria tray.

Sierra felt as if the world had suddenly turned against her.

How could her friends not understand? Why was all of this her fault?

"You guys," Margo said, clearing her throat and talking a little louder. "We should all back down like Tre did. Don't give Sierra a hard time." Margo rose and said, "Excuse me. I better tell Drake we're all uninvited."

"You're not uninvited," Sierra said, dreading how this would sound to Drake. "I still need to talk to my brother. Can you guys wait until tomorrow for a final decision? This isn't supposed to be such a huge problem."

"I guess you can blame me for that," Vicki said quietly. The sweet bloom of innocence no longer graced her face. "I didn't mean to turn this into a nightmare."

"I know. You didn't do anything wrong on purpose." Sierra glanced at Randy, hoping he would say something to help smooth everyone's ruffled feelings.

He stuffed the last bite of his sandwich into his mouth and said, "If you hear from Wes tonight, call me. I'd still like to invite myself, if that's okay with you and Wes."

Sierra wanted to say, "Yes, of course. I'm sure Wes would love to have you come." But how would that look to Warner and the others?

"I'll call you," Sierra said. She knew she would call Randy whether she heard from Wes or not. Then they could have a private conversation about all this.

True to her word, Sierra called Randy as soon as she arrived home. But she got his family's answering machine, so she tried Wes. Fortunately, Wes was there.

After explaining the situation, Sierra asked her brother what he thought she should do. There was a pause on the other end, and Sierra wondered if Wes was thinking the same thing her dad had voiced the night before: *Only you, Sierra!*

"I think this should be a fun trip for you, Sierra," Wes began. "And I also think it's an opportunity to do something nice for your friends. You should consider that."

"What do you mean?"

"Turn the situation around. What if Randy were going on a trip like this, and he invited two of the people from your group but didn't invite you. How would you feel?"

"It's not as though we're an inseparable group that does everything together," Sierra protested. "Those guys go off and do stuff without me all the time. Besides, I invited Amy, and she doesn't even attend our school anymore. I wanted it to be a girlfriend trip. It changes the whole atmosphere when guys are around."

"Uh, Sierra," Wes said slowly, "I'm a guy."

"I know, but . . ." Now Sierra didn't know what to say. Wes was right. Already the possibility existed that the atmosphere would be charged because of Amy's potential interest in Wes. Maybe Sierra's dream of what this trip was supposed to be was unrealistic.

"Look, Sierra, I don't know what to tell you. I'm open to taking more of your friends if that would be helpful to them and if that's something you would like. The point of this trip is for me to check out Rancho Corona and for you to look over some colleges. It's not about going to the beach or Hollywood or wherever else your friends want to go. Maybe, if you make the schedule really clear, some of them will change their minds. We won't have a lot of time to see the sights."

"I know," Sierra said with a sigh. "You're right. I should think of what would be good for my friends. It's just that I don't like being around Warner."

"Then don't invite Warner."

"But you just said to open the invitation to all of them."

"It's up to you, Sierra."

"You're not much help. First you tell me one thing, then you change it."

"I'm not changing anything. Listen, Sierra, this is what you should do. Make a rough schedule based on the colleges you, Vicki, and Amy want to visit. Then, if there's time, we'll fit in one fun thing, like the beach or something. Show that schedule to your friends, tell them they have to pay for their food, and then see who still wants to come. If Randy wants to come, I'd be glad for the company."

"What about Warner?"

"What about him?"

Sierra curled and uncurled her toes. She felt her jaw clenching. "Wesley, help me out here. I don't want Warner to come."

"Okay, then use me as your excuse. Tell Warner he can't come because I said so."

"But you don't even know him."

"You're right; I don't. You know him. You tell him he can't come."

Sierra let out an exasperated sigh. Obviously, no easy answer was going to turn up. "What about sleeping? Won't it be impossible to stretch out and sleep with so many people in the van?"

"We'll take turns sleeping in the front seat. It reclines. You can sleep on an airplane, can't you? You can sleep in the van."

Sierra bit her lower lip until she was afraid she might draw blood. "I'm going to hang up on you now, Wesley, and don't try to call me back. I can't handle any more of your wacky logic."

"Okay. Let me know what you decide." He seemed untouched by her frustration.

"I will," Sierra muttered. She hung up and headed for the basement to find her mom.

Mrs. Jensen was pulling clothes from the washing machine and stuffing them into the dryer. Sierra blurted out her problem and waited expectantly for her mother to wave a magic sheet of fabric softener to make all the static go away.

Instead, her mom leaned against the dryer and said, "So, what are you going to do?"

This was the part about entering adulthood Sierra disliked the most. Her parents let her make most of her own decisions. They said she would grow more if she learned from the consequences and rewards of her own choices. It drove Sierra crazy! Her parents seemed to find a strange parental satisfaction in putting the responsibility back on her.

"I don't know yet."

"Is Warner a difficult person to get along with?" her mom asked.

"He doesn't seem to annoy other people as much as he bugs me. He used to come up and put his arm around my shoulder. He's so tall it felt as though he was hanging on me and trying to make people think we were together or something."

"Does he still do that?"

"No. I made it clear awhile ago I didn't like it, and he finally stopped. Now he's kind of mean to me. He says cutting things and gives me these nasty looks."

Mrs. Jensen smiled.

"What?" Sierra asked.

"If you were in junior high, I'd say Warner had a pretty serious crush on you."

"Exactly! That's what makes it so annoying. We're not in junior high; we're seniors in high school! Why can't he act normal?"

"Some guys take a little longer than others to mature. You know that. Don't confuse immaturity with meanness."

"But, Mom, tell me, on a trip like this do you think I have to invite someone who is immature just to be nice to him?"

"I don't know," Mrs. Jensen said thoughtfully. "A trip like this might help him grow up."

Sierra lifted her hands in a pleading gesture to her mother. "Why is it suddenly my responsibility to make sure Warner gets a life? And why is this trip about Warner? It was supposed to be a fun, fact-finding time for Wes and me, and then I included Amy and Vicki. That was it. A nice, cozy little package. Why can't it be like that?"

"What about Randy?"

"Okay, Wes, Amy, Vicki, Randy, and me." As soon as Sierra verbalized the guest list, she realized it sounded like two couples: Wes and Amy, Vicki and Randy. Sierra would be the leftover—unless Warner came, and that would make everything worse. She hadn't even considered Margo in all the deliberations. What if Margo and Warner both came, and they ended up being a couple? Three couples with Sierra as the outsider.

"I'm getting a headache," Sierra said. "I'm going up to my room. I told Randy I'd call him."

"Could you carry this basket of laundry up to the kitchen for me?" Mrs. Jensen asked.

"Sure." Sierra bent down to pick up the wicker basket by the side handles.

"Oh, and by the way," Mrs. Jensen said, "did you see the letter that came for you? It's on the chair in the study."

chapter five

UST THE THOUGHT OF A LETTER WAITING FOR HER LIGHT-
ened Sierra's load. She put the laundry basket on the
kitchen counter and hurried to her favorite spot. Lift-
ing the envelope and skimming the bold, black letters that
spelled her name on the front, Sierra smiled. Something
inside her always stirred like a breeze across a meadow when
she held a letter from Paul.

Settling in her chair and carefully opening the letter, Sierra
began to read:

> *Dear Sierra,*
>
> *Well, I've finally made some decisions. It's taken a long
> time, and I've sure gone through my share of inner torture
> trying to discern God's direction. I couldn't have made it
> without your prayer support. Thank you!*

Sierra looked up and swallowed hard. She knew all
about making decisions and the inner torture one could go
through. Paul's words made her realize she hadn't prayed
about her own situation. It seemed ironic she was able to
help Paul make some decisions with her encouragement
and prayer support; yet who did she have praying for her?
And why wasn't she talking over her struggles with God?

Returning her thoughts and attention to Paul's letter, she read on.

> *I'm not sure if I told you how they break down the academic terms at the university. The spring term ends next week. We have a month-long break, and then what they call the summer term begins; it goes from the middle of April to the middle of June. I'll be staying for the summer term, and then it looks as though I'll be returning to the States.*

Sierra felt a rush of hope and anticipation at the thought of Paul's coming home. He had gone to school in Portland the year before, but his family lived in San Diego, where his dad was a pastor. Would Paul return to Portland, or would he go to college elsewhere? She read on.

> *As you know, it's been hard for me to work through this decision. When I came over here, I thought I'd finish out my degree at the University of Edinburgh. That had been my goal since my sophomore year in high school. I wanted to leave home and be with my grandfather. As you know, he died before I was able to come to school here. The entrance requirements were that I had at least one year at a qualifying university in the U.S., which is how I ended up at Lewis and Clark College.*
> *Anyway, I came over thinking that I could help my grandmother and that the University of Edinburgh would be everything I had dreamed of when I first visited the campus as a 15-year-old. The truth is, my grandmother is quite self-sufficient and has made it clear it has become a bother for me to impose on her hospitality every weekend. I've made a few friends at the school, but not real close friends, since I haven't stayed around on*

weekends. The classes have been great, and I believe this year has been a good experience for me in many ways, especially in getting my heart set back on the Lord. There's a rugged loneliness about this country that makes a heart cry out. I'm grateful that when I sought the Lord, He heard me and came close.

As for my future plans, those are still formulating. When I first asked you to pray about this with me, I was considering coming home at the end of the spring term in March, but it was to my benefit to take the classes offered from April to June. I have a month off before those classes begin, so I'm going to do some traveling. I'd like to check out a sailing camp on the northwest coast of Scotland. Then I think I'll come back down to Stranraer and take the Sea Cat Hydrofoil over to Belfast.

Again Sierra stopped reading and let her imagination drift with Paul's words. Sierra had been to Belfast more than a year ago. She would have to write Paul right away to tell him to visit The Giant's Causeway on the north coast. Sierra remembered how fascinated she had been with this natural work of God where the lava had flowed into the sea long ago and hardened into extremely large, steplike blocks of rocks. It did indeed look like a cobblestone path for giants.

I'd appreciate your prayers for safety while I travel and for all the decisions that still need to be made about what I'll do when I leave here in June. I need to close for now. There's a big rugby tournament at Murrayfield Stadium this afternoon. Scotland vs. France. You probably know that rugby is the sport over here. This game promises to be a good one and worth the study break I'm taking to see it.

Hope everything is going well for you. Thanks again

for all your prayers and encouragement. I don't think you'll ever know how much they mean to me.

> *With a grateful heart,*
> *Paul*

As soon as she read Paul's signature, Sierra turned back to the first page of onionskin paper and started to read every word over again. That's what she usually did when she received a letter from Paul.

She had almost finished the letter for the second time when the phone rang. Mrs. Jensen answered it and called for Sierra, telling her Randy was on the line.

Carefully folding Paul's letter and tucking it back into the envelope, Sierra reached for the phone on her dad's desk. "Hi ya," she answered cheerfully.

Randy paused a moment and then said, "You sound as if you're in a better mood than you were at lunch. Does that mean you've talked to your brother?"

Sierra's cheeks flushed. She felt as though she had been caught in a private moment of interacting with Paul. She would have experienced the same sort of embarrassment if she and Paul had been together, here in the study, sitting close and looking warmly into each other's eyes, and then the door burst open and Randy barged in.

"Yes, I've talked to Wes," Sierra began, pulling together her thoughts. "I'm not sure I have a real clear direction yet, but he did say he would like it if you came along."

"Cool," Randy said. "I'm in. I got someone to do my Saturday lawn jobs for me. By the way, my parents want to know which colleges we're going to visit, and I want to know how much money you think I should bring."

Sierra listed the colleges and then told him that he would

have to cover all his meals and that they would only do something fun if there was enough time in the schedule.

"Okay," Randy said. "My parents also want me to chip in some money for the gas, so I figured I'd give Wesley 50 bucks, unless you think I should give him more."

"That sounds like a lot," Sierra said.

"My dad said it's way less than an airline ticket."

"Randy, do you think Warner and Margo would still want to go if they knew we weren't sure about making it to the beach or some other fun place? I mean, are they serious about this being a college scouting trip?"

"I don't know. I think so. Drake wanted to know if we were going to swing over to the coast. He wanted to check out Westridge in Santa Barbara."

Drake! Sierra felt the panic rising again. The last bit of euphoria she had felt over Paul's letter vanished when Randy reminded her about Drake. She had forgotten about his wanting to go. Or maybe she had pushed that thought far away when she became upset over Warner.

"The thing is, it's going to be really crowded, Randy. Who do you think should go? I mean, it's definitely you, Wes, Vicki, Amy, and me. Only three more seats are in the van, if we figure enough room for everyone's luggage. If Drake, Warner, and Margo all go, I think it's going to be too crowded for such a long trip."

"Could be. I don't know. You're going to have to call the shots."

"I wish everyone would stop telling me that!" Sierra blurted out. "Do you know how frustrating it is to suddenly be responsible for all this? This trip was supposed to be nice and easy, but now it's turned into a popularity contest or something."

Randy didn't say anything.

"I mean, how would you feel if you had to make these choices?"

"I don't know. I'd probably figure out what works best for the whole trip, and if I had to tell some people there wasn't room, I'd tell them. I don't think it would hurt your friendship with anyone. Everybody understands the situation, Sierra."

"You understand because you're definitely going. What if you were one of the ones I said no to?"

"I'd understand," Randy said without hesitation.

"Yeah, well, you're Randy. You always understand. What about the others?"

"If they're really your friends, your decision won't change that."

"I don't know, Randy. They would probably say if I was really their friend there wouldn't be any discussion. I'd want them all to come."

"Maybe."

Sierra was beginning to get the same dull headache she had felt when she talked to Wes earlier in the evening.

"Do me a favor and don't say anything about going until after lunch tomorrow, okay, Randy?"

"Okay."

"I'm going to pray about all this, and then we can settle everything tomorrow."

"Whatever," Randy said.

"Right," Sierra agreed, feeling as ambivalent as Randy's comment. "Whatever."

chapter six

N WEDNESDAY AFTERNOON, THE DAY OF THE COLLEGE scouting trip, Sierra stood in the driveway watching her father tighten the luggage rack on top of the van. Randy was in the front yard, tossing a stick for Brutus, the Jensen family dog. Amy had run into the house to use the bathroom, and Vicki stood next to Sierra.

Sierra was listening to Vicki, but her glare was fixed on Warner, who already had claimed the front passenger seat of the van and now sat there like a rock.

"I wonder if Drake dropped out at the last minute because he found out Margo wasn't going," Vicki said quietly. "I've noticed they've been hanging around together this past week or so."

"Could be," Sierra muttered. When Margo's parents found out Sierra's brother, and not her parents, was chaperoning the trip, they decided Margo couldn't go. Then at lunch today Drake had come up to Sierra and simply said he had changed his mind because he had "too much going on."

Ever since Sierra had made her big decision and announced a week ago that Randy, Warner, Drake, and Margo were all welcome to come, she silently had hoped Drake and Warner wouldn't go—especially Warner. So when Drake dropped out at the last minute, Sierra couldn't help but wish Warner would do the same.

But no, Warner was going. There he was, planted in the front seat. Sierra kept reminding herself of all the pointers her mom had mentioned the night before about Sierra's setting boundaries with him and reinforcing them whenever necessary. Mrs. Jensen also had reminded Sierra this might be the kind of experience that would have a positive, maturing effect on Warner, and she had praised Sierra for being mature enough to include him even when it wasn't her preference.

Sierra felt anything but mature at the moment. She didn't want to be responsible for driving the family van 100 miles down to Corvallis with Randy, Warner, Amy, and Vicki depending on her. Sierra would have felt much more comfortable if her dad stepped in and volunteered to drive them to Wesley's. But she knew her dad wouldn't; he trusted her, and her friends depended on her. She never would have expected it, but being mature and responsible on such occasions was a troublesome, nerve-wracking condition.

Putting on her best smile, Sierra thanked her dad for loading the luggage rack.

"I filled the tank and checked the oil this morning," Mr. Jensen said as he handed Sierra the keys. "Remind Wes to check the oil again before you start the return trip."

"I will."

"And call us when you get to Wesley's," Mrs. Jensen said.

"I will."

"Make sure everyone wears seat belts," Mr. Jensen said. "I took out an umbrella insurance policy so you're all covered in case anything happens. But make sure you're always driving the speed limit, obeying the traffic laws, and all wearing seat belts."

"Okay," Sierra agreed. "We will." Her parents' last-minute instructions were beginning to make her even more nervous. "I'm sure we'll be fine."

"That's what we're praying," Mrs. Jensen said. "You have a good time and call if there are any problems."

"We will." Sierra reached over to open the van door in an attempt to get going. Mrs. Jensen caught Sierra before she could climb into the van, and with a big hug, she kissed her on the cheek. Her mom's demonstration embarrassed Sierra. "Bye," Sierra said quickly, clambering into the van.

"Good-bye," Mr. Jensen called out. Fortunately, he had not tried to give Sierra a kiss in front of her friends. She felt a twinge of shame over how her parents' loving intentions were embarrassing to her.

Amy and Vicki climbed into the bench seat behind Sierra, and Randy went to the seat behind them, carrying his bulky guitar case with him.

"Seat belts on, everyone," Mr. Jensen called out. To Sierra's relief, all of them obliged without saying anything.

"Everybody ready?" Sierra asked as she started the engine. Sierra was surprised to find she didn't like being in the driver's seat or being in charge. Since her earliest years she had been told she was a natural leader. Maybe she felt awkward leading her peers. Or maybe she felt self-conscious with her parents standing there in the driveway with their arms around each other, waving at her wistfully, as if she were going out to sea for a dangerous voyage and they might never see her again. Wherever the uncomfortable feeling came from, it began to diminish by the time they were on the freeway heading south to Corvallis.

"Anybody want some gum?" Vicki offered.

"What kind is it?" Warner asked.

"Spearmint. Do you want some?"

"No way. I only chew bubble gum," Warner said. "Which reminds me, I forgot to bring some. Pull off the freeway at the next exit, Sierra. I need to buy some gum."

"I'm not getting off for gum," Sierra said. The extra sharp edge to her words surprised even her. It was quiet for a minute. "I told my parents we were driving straight through," she added, trying to soften her tone. "You can wait until we reach Corvallis to buy some gum, can't you?"

Warner lifted his long legs and rested his feet on the dashboard. He looked like a scrunched-up grasshopper. "Guess I don't have much choice."

"Could you put your feet down?" Sierra asked.

"Make me," Warner taunted.

"Warner, your legs are blocking my view of the side mirror."

"No they're not."

"Warner," Sierra said, losing what tiny shreds of patience she had left, "put your legs down! This is my parents' van, and my dad doesn't like people to put their feet on the dash like that."

"Your dad's not here, is he?"

"It's still his car," Sierra said. "So I'm telling you, put your legs down!"

Warner slowly lowered his feet and turned to stare at Sierra. "Are you going to be this much fun the whole trip?"

"I don't know. Are you going to be this big of a jerk?"

The other passengers remained silent.

"I'm sorry," Sierra said. "That wasn't very kind. Let's start over, Warner, okay? All I'm saying is that my parents have put a lot of trust in me for this trip, and I want to honor them. Can you support me in this?"

"Sure," Warner said with a shrug. "You're the woman. You run the tour. I'm only along for the wild ride."

Sierra couldn't help but think Warner had no idea what a wild ride this was for her emotions. She was fully aware that what she hadn't wanted to happen was happening. Warner was coming on this trip, and she had blown up at him within the first 20 minutes. Sierra also knew that once they picked up Wesley, they would be a traveling band of six. Three guys and three girls. Matched up, that meant Vicki and Randy, Amy and Wes, and Warner and her. The thought made Sierra's stomach turn. From now until Sunday night she would have to fight her aggressive dislike for Warner.

Why is this so hard, God? she prayed. *What's my problem? I thought I'd worked through all this and decided to be kind and loving to everyone the way You want me to be. I'm sorry, but this is impossible.*

"Do you want some gum, Sierra?" Vicki rather timidly held out a stick as a peace offering.

"Sure. Thanks."

Warner pulled a skateboarding magazine out of the gym bag he had smashed into the space between his seat and the driver's. He also took out a Walkman and placed the headset into his ears. For the next 45 minutes he kept in his own little world, tapping his fingers on the dashboard in time to the headset music.

Warner also appeared to have brought a stash of junk food in his gym bag because he kept reaching in for more snacks. First he downed a can of soda, crushed the can, and dropped it on the van's floor. Then he ate a bag of popcorn, leaving bits of kernels everywhere. The large bag of M&M's was devoured without Warner's offering any to anyone else. He tossed the empty bag onto the floor on Sierra's side of the

van, since his side was full. Then he went for a bag of bar-
becue-flavored corn nuts, which smelled up the whole van.

During Warner's pig-out session, Randy sat in the backseat quietly playing his guitar. Sierra, Amy, and Vicki tried to
ignore Warner and talked about some of their expectations
of the different colleges and other bits of information they
each had gathered during the week. It wasn't the same level
of girl chat they shared at Mama Bear's every week, since they
knew two guys could listen in at any time. But Sierra was
encouraged that Amy and Vicki had both gotten into the
spirit of the trip.

"I have some coupons my uncle gave me for Magic
Mountain," Amy said. "I don't know if they're any good, but
it says they can be used at any of the Six Flags Amusement
Parks."

"For what? Free admission?" Vicki asked.

"No, I think it's something like six dollars off the admission price."

"My mom gave me a AAA guidebook to Southern California. It lists all the hours and admission prices for the
different amusement parks and stuff," Vicki said. "I know
we're not really planning on going anywhere specific, but if
we decide to, at least we have some information."

"That's great," Sierra said. "I'm sure something will work
out. It'll be spontaneous, though."

"That's the best kind of fun," Vicki said.

Just outside of Salem, light rain began to fall. Sierra turned
on the wiper blades and slowed down. The traffic seemed to
be thickening, now that it was getting close to 5:00.

"You know what, Sierra?" Vicki leaned forward to speak,
but it was impossible to have a confidential conversation with
Warner planted there in the passenger seat. "I know we're

supposed to go straight through to Corvallis, but I need to make a bathroom stop. I don't think I can wait. Would it be okay if we stopped?"

"Sure," Sierra said.

Warner looked up from his magazine and pulled the headset from his ears. "Oh, we're going to stop, are we? May I please get out of the car, too, Miss Tour Queen? Please, oh please?"

"Warner, why do you have to be like that?" Vicki snapped.

Warner tossed the empty bag of corn nuts at Vicki and said, "Think fast."

Sierra checked the rearview mirror for Vicki's reaction.

To her credit, Vicki remained composed. "You're acting like a jerk, Warner. Why don't you cut it out?"

"What is it with all the females in this wagon?" Warner mocked.

"Don't go there, Warner," Randy warned from the backseat. It was the first time he had said anything since they had left. Sierra was surprised at his outburst, but she appreciated her friend's support.

Sierra didn't say anything. She put on her turn signal and carefully made the lane change to exit the freeway. At the first gas station on the right, she pulled in and parked to the side, near the door to the rest room.

"I'll be right back," Vicki said.

"I'm going with you," Sierra said.

"Me, too," Amy said, sliding out the side door behind Vicki.

"It's a law of nature," Warner said, loud enough for them all to hear. "All females of the species go to the bathroom in herds." Only Warner laughed.

"Here, Randy," Sierra said, tossing him the keys. "You're on guard duty."

Sierra followed Amy and Vicki into the rest room. As soon as the door was shut behind them, the three of them started talking.

"I can't do this," Vicki said. "I didn't think he would be this bad. He's going to drive me crazy!"

"Why did you invite him, Sierra?" Amy asked.

"I didn't exactly want to," Sierra said, giving Vicki a sideways glance. Quickly realizing this was no time to start placing blame, Sierra quietly added, "It was very complicated. Trust me on this, you guys. I prayed long and hard over it, and I thought I was doing the right thing by opening up the invitation to him."

"Nice to him, maybe. But it's not nice for us to have to put up with him," Amy said.

"It's not going to work," Vicki said. "We have to figure out what we can do about this. He's going to make the whole trip miserable for everyone. I thought I was going to pass out from the smell of those corn nuts."

"No kidding," Amy said.

"We could try to set boundaries with him," Sierra offered. "That's what my mom suggested. We could tell him when and how he's irritating us and ask him to stop doing those things."

"Do you really think that will work?" Amy asked.

"Everything he's doing irritates me," Vicki said.

"I know." Sierra washed her hands and looked at her reflection in the mirror. Her hair was beginning to frizz the way it always did in the rain. Tiny ringlets had already tightened at her temples.

"All I know is that we can't go on this way for the whole

trip." Vicki joined Sierra at the sink and washed her hands. She also gave herself a quick exam in the mirror. "Oh, I hate my hair," she muttered.

"Don't even get Sierra started on that subject," Amy's voice called from behind the closed stall door. "Stick to the subject of Warner. What are we going to do about him?"

Vicki and Sierra looked at each other and at the same time said, "Scream!"

chapter seven

THE THREE FRIENDS STAYED IN THE REST ROOM WITH the door locked long enough to come up with a plan. Before they drove another inch, they were going to confront Warner. They would tell him what was bothering them and ask him to try to be considerate of everyone else on the trip. If these three friends had learned one thing, it was that the right way to handle a conflict was to go to the person you have the problem with and talk it over with him in a kind manner. They only hoped it would work with Warner.

When they finally returned to the van, Randy appeared to be having his own little "correctional conversation" with Warner in the backseat. None of the trash around Warner's seat had been removed.

As soon as Sierra opened the door on the driver's side, Warner turned to her and said, "Randy says I'm making everybody mad."

Sierra looked at Randy and then at Amy and Vicki, who were standing by the open sliding side door, waiting to get in.

Amy entered the van and looked at Warner. "I don't know what your expectations were of this trip, but I know for the est of us we were expecting to have a good time. When you

44

act pushy, rude, and inconsiderate of everyone else, it's hard to feel like we're having a good time. It also makes it impossible for everyone to get along."

Warner looked stumped. "Why are you guys all against me?"

"We're not," three of them said in unison. Sierra was the only one who didn't pipe up.

"It's like I was trying to explain to you, Warner," Randy said. "When you're part of a group or on a team, everyone looks out for everyone else and tries to consider other people's feelings first. Making rude comments or being sarcastic doesn't build any kind of unity."

"I'm only kidding," Warner said. "Why can't you guys take a joke? Why is everyone so uptight?"

Sierra began to wonder if her dislike of Warner had rubbed off on the others and they were now taking her side and trying to reform Warner in three easy steps to make him more acceptable to Sierra. If she honestly were a team player, as Randy said, and if she had considered Warner's feelings, she wouldn't have thrown the first stone by snapping at him about not stopping until they reached Corvallis.

And look, she thought, *we stopped after all. So my statement was worthless.*

"You guys," Sierra said, "I don't think I've exactly been a terrific team player. I was rude to you, Warner, and I apologize."

Warner looked at each of them and shrugged his thin shoulders. "Okay. Can we get going?"

"Okay," Sierra said, reaching across the seat for the keys Randy held out to her.

Vicki opened the passenger door and started to get in the front seat.

"Whoa!" Warner said, crawling out of the backseat of the van. "That's my seat."

"Your seat?" Vicki said, picking up the empty snack bags and stuffing them into the litter bag hanging from the glove compartment. "And is this your trash, too? I say whoever picks up the trash gets to ride in the front. It's not very far to Corvallis."

"I take the front," Warner said, motioning for Vicki to move with an aggressive jerk of his thumb. "I get carsick unless I ride in the front seat."

Sierra glanced at Amy, whose dark eyes grew wide. Vicki's face took on the same look of disbelief.

"You mean you expect to ride in the front seat all the way to California and back?" Vicki said, still not moving from the seat.

"Unless you want me to barf all over everyone in the back."

Vicki quietly exited and took her seat next to Amy on the middle bench. Warner scrambled in and closed the door with a slam that Sierra knew would have prompted her dad to say, "Not so hard. You'll break it."

Instead, Sierra said, "Warner, why did you want to come on this trip?"

"What do you mean?"

"I mean, I'd like to know what your idea of a road trip is?"

"This," he said. "Why?"

Vicki leaned forward. "Have you ever gone anywhere with friends before?"

"The band went up to Longview a couple of months ago."

"Longview," Amy repeated. "That's like 40 miles away. You've never traveled with friends or family before?"

Warner shook his head. "No. What's the big deal? I wanted to come because everyone else was coming."

"Not everyone," Vicki said. "Tre couldn't come. Margo and Drake decided not to come. I don't understand why you wanted to."

"Do I need to spell it out?"

"Yes, if you could," Sierra said calmly. "It would help."

"Because I hang out with you guys," Warner said in a monotone.

"You're saying we're your friends?" Vicki asked. "'Cause if that's what you're saying, Warner, then you need to treat us a whole lot nicer than you have been. Friends don't treat friends the way you're treating us."

"She has a point," Randy said. "You need a little work in that area, buddy. We're all willing to hang in there with you, but come on. You have to move our way a little, too. I mean, try to be a team player here. That's all we're saying."

Warner still looked as if he just didn't get it. Sierra gave up and started the van. "Let's get back on the road. Wes is going to wonder what happened to us." Secretly, she hoped that Wes would turn out to be the ideal referee for this volatile group of team players and that he could talk some consideration into Warner.

They arrived in Corvallis without any complications, mostly because Sierra ignored Warner and then focused on finding her way to where Wes lived. They located the house he shared with several other college guys, and Sierra parked the van in the church parking lot next to the old, two-story house, just as her dad had instructed her. Wes came out to greet them before they even made it up the stairs to the front door. The sight of her dear, older brother had a calming effect on Sierra.

Wes physically resembled their dad, especially his eyes, which were a warm brown color; and he had the same brown, wavy hair as their dad, except that Wes had a full head of hair and no receding hairline. He was over six feet tall, which comforted Sierra, because by virtue of size alone Warner was no longer the biggest of their group.

"Why don't you go in and call Mom?" Wes suggested. "I'm not quite ready. It might be a good idea for you guys to hang out here and stretch your legs awhile."

Sierra noticed that Warner immediately returned to the van. She guessed he was retrieving his skateboard, which he had stuck under the middle seat. As she walked up the steps to the front door with Wes, she began quietly to tell her brother about the conflict with Warner on the way down.

"I've done everything I can think of," Sierra said as they entered the living room. "First, I invited him. That was nice. When he was rude, I snapped at him, but then I apologized. We all talked to him about being a team player, but he just doesn't get it. He says he has to ride in the front seat the entire trip or he'll get sick."

Wesley's eyebrows rose. Being from a large family, Wes and Sierra had learned early on to share whatever they had and to be considerate of others. That included "dibs" on the shotgun seat. Everyone took a turn.

"Do you want me to tell him I don't want him to come?" Wes asked.

"How can you tell him that? He's already here."

"We could take him back to Portland. Or we could put him on a bus back, or call his parents and tell them it's not going to work out for him to come."

Sierra sighed. "I don't know. Here I thought I was solving the problem by not excluding him, and now it's worse because I invited him. I should have said no in the beginning and let him be mad at me."

"You prayed about it, didn't you?" Wes asked.

"Yes, I sincerely did."

"Then you have to go on faith at this point. You have to believe he's here for a reason."

"Does that mean he has to stay?" Sierra asked.

"Not necessarily." Wes glanced at his watch. "Why don't you call Mom and Dad? Let them know you arrived, and I'll see if my clothes are finished in the dryer so I can pack."

"You haven't started to pack?"

"It will take me only a few minutes," Wes promised as he headed for the back of the house.

Sierra called home and chose to tell her parents only that the group had arrived safely and there had been no problems with the van. She didn't want to bring up the Warner issue. "We did make one stop, though, outside of Salem. Vicki had to go to the rest room. I guess Wes is finishing his packing, and then we're leaving. I'll call you tomorrow when I have a chance." Sierra knew her parents hadn't asked her to call regularly to check in. She also knew they would really like it if she did.

"Great," Mrs. Jensen said. "Have a wonderful time. We're praying for you."

Sierra hung up, feeling a little more optimistic. Wes was in the driver's seat now, so to speak. He would take over and work things out. He would also be the responsible one in case anything went wrong. It was a position Sierra gladly relinquished.

She was about to head back outside when Amy came rushing in through the front door. "Sierra, come quick! It's Warner! Tell Wes to come."

"What happened?"

"Warner ran into a truck!"

chapter eight

"WARNER WAS RIDING HIS SKATEBOARD," AMY breathlessly explained as Sierra and Wes jogged with her down the street, "and this truck came around the corner. Warner caught up with it and grabbed the back bumper. Then the truck put on its brakes at the stop sign."

"And Warner crashed into the back of the truck," Sierra concluded as they arrived at the scene of the accident. Warner was splayed out on the street. A dozen people had gathered around him.

"He thinks he broke his arm," Vicki said. "One of the guys here already called the paramedics."

Sierra noticed that Warner's right arm was twisted in a scarecrow-like position, and he was grimacing. She knew it wasn't very nice, but her first thought was to scold him by saying, "What were you thinking? Didn't you even consider it might be dangerous?"

The paramedics arrived and carted Warner off to the hospital. Sierra was thankful Wesley was there to take over the job of calling Warner's parents and explaining what had happened. Warner's mom got directions to the hospital from Wes and urged them to go ahead and leave for their trip. She said that even if Warner's arm weren't broken, he couldn't continue the trip with them. As Wes relayed it, Warner's mom said that if Warner was going to take risks like that and not act responsibly, then he couldn't enjoy the privilege of going on the trip. Apparently, the last thing Warner's mom said to Wes was, "His father and I were so hoping this trip would be a breakthrough for him. Warner has never been good at friendships or responsibility."

"I didn't want something bad to happen to him," Sierra said as the solemn group of five pulled into the hospital parking lot.

"Don't start blaming yourself," Vicki said quickly. "It was an accident, and it happened because Warner was being a daredevil and showing off. It had nothing to do with any of us."

"I know what Sierra means, though," Amy added. "I can't help but feel bad, too."

"Come on," Wes said, turning off the van's engine. "We'll buy him some balloons and tell him we hope he feels better. That's the best we can do. It's all we can do."

"Are you going to tell him his mom said he can't continue on the trip?" Sierra asked.

"Unless you want to."

"No thank you," Sierra said.

After a stop at the hospital gift shop, Wes led them into the emergency room and the area where Warner was lying in bed.

"They told me it broke in two places," Warner moaned when he saw them. "The doctor showed me the X-rays. I can't believe the idiot in that truck stopped so suddenly."

"Idiot in the truck?" Vicki spouted. "Warner, you were the one who shouldn't have been holding on to the bumper!

What did you think would happen?" She stood the farthest from the bed and placed her hand on her hip.

"I've done it before, and nothing ever happened."

"Here," Sierra said, tying the string from the get-well balloons to the metal railing of Warner's bed. "These are to cheer you up."

"Thanks. But don't you think they'll be too much of a distraction for you in the van?"

"Warner," Wes said, "your mom is coming. She said she didn't want you to go the rest of the way. She's taking you home."

Warner looked stunned. "Why?"

"She will have to talk that through with you," Wes said.

"Did you tell her to come get me?"

"Nope. I called her and told her what had happened, and she told me exactly what I've relayed to you." Wes looked at his watch. "She'll probably be here within the next hour and a half. We can stay here with you, if you'd like."

Warner looked depressed. For a fraction of a second, Sierra almost felt sorry for him. "No," he finally said, his head down. "You guys need to get on the road. I don't want to hold you back."

"That's really considerate of you," Randy said. "We appreciate it."

"I'm sorry this happened to you," Sierra said, giving Warner a weak but sincere smile.

"We all are," Amy added. "I hope it doesn't hurt too much."

"I'll be okay. You guys just go."

"Thanks, Warner," Wes said. "I'll get your stuff from the van and bring it back in here for you."

Warner nodded and gave a weak wave to the rest of them.

"I'll put your card right here," Sierra said, opening the

envelope for him and laying the get-well card on his leg. "Take it easy, okay?"

Warner met her gaze with a more settled look than she had ever seen on his long face. It almost seemed as if he had grown up a little bit.

Sierra and the others were back in the van and 20 miles down the freeway before they started to talk about Warner. They needed that much time to process their thoughts and feelings.

"Do you think God lets bad things happen so that good things come out of it?" Vicki asked. "Like, I mean, what if this broken arm turns into a real humbling and growing experience for Warner? What if the lessons he learns from the broken arm are more valuable than the lessons he would have learned on this trip with us?"

"You mean the lessons we would have tried to cram down his throat," Sierra said. "That's my problem. I'm so quick to see where I think people are wrong and need to change, and then, just because it seems obvious to me, I think they should see it, too, and instantly desire to change."

"At least you care enough to want to see your friends improve," Randy said. "That's not a bad thing, Sierra."

"Unless she crams it down your throat, as she said," Amy added.

Sierra looked at Amy, who was now seated in the front passenger seat, next to Wes. Amy didn't turn to meet Sierra's gaze, but Sierra knew exactly what Amy was thinking. "I know, I know," Sierra said. "My track record for tact and gentleness aren't that great. You've had to endure the brunt of that, Amy. I hope I'm getting a little better at being a good friend."

"Yeah, as long as we keep all air horns away from you," Amy said.

Sierra cringed. The air horn had to be one of her silliest moves. In an effort to show Amy she was on her side, last fall Sierra had followed Amy and her old boyfriend, Nathan, as they left The Beet, a local teen night spot. When Sierra saw Nathan grab Amy's shoulders, she had sounded an air horn behind him to give Amy a chance to run away. Only Amy had had no need of Sierra's assistance and so didn't run anywhere. Sierra still couldn't believe she had done that.

"At least you admit when you're wrong," Vicki said. "That quality in and of itself makes you a good friend. My problem is I'm so afraid people will get mad at me or decide they no longer like me that I have a hard time admitting I'm wrong."

"Not always," Sierra said.

"Maybe not in the last eight months or so, ever since summer camp when I got my life back on track with God. But before then, I never willingly would admit I was wrong. Isn't that right, Amy?"

"I'm staying out of this."

"Well, it's true," Vicki said. "But that's all in the past, and it's all been forgiven, right?"

"Right," Sierra said when no one else spoke up.

"We need to move on," Vicki said. "Move on in our friendships and move on now that Warner isn't with us. We can't spend the whole trip feeling responsible."

"Right," Sierra added again.

"It does feel different, though, doesn't it?" Vicki said. "I mean, it feels like a completely different trip than the first two hours when we had Warner and didn't have Wes."

"Are you saying you made a good trade?" Wes said with a sly grin at Vicki in the rearview mirror.

"Definitely," Amy said. "No offense, you guys, but I'm so relieved Warner isn't going any farther with us. He would have been a pain the whole time."

"I think it feels more peaceful now," Sierra said. "Is that how you guys feel? It's much calmer."

"That's because Randy is asleep back there," Wes said, glancing again in the mirror.

Randy mimicked loud snoring noises from the backseat.

"Randy is just being his usual, peacemaking self and not saying much," Vicki observed.

"Snoring like that isn't going to make a lot of peace with me at night, I can tell you that," Wes said.

"Oh, right," Sierra jumped in. "You snore much worse than that, Wes, and I have proof."

"Anyone else getting hungry?" Wes asked. "I need to buy some gas, so we might as well eat, too."

"Don't try to change the subject," Sierra teased her brother. "You might as well confess to everyone now, since we're going to be in close quarters for a long time. They'll find out sooner or later."

"Okay, okay, I snore like a chain saw. There. Now you all know."

"Gavin even recorded him this Christmas to show him how loud he snores."

"He turned up the volume on the recorder," Wes said, putting on his turn signal and moving into the slow lane.

"He did not! That's exactly how you sound," Sierra said.

"Any preferences on where we stop for dinner?"

"Anywhere. Except maybe not Burger King," Vicki said. "I had Burger King last night."

"I had McDonald's for lunch," Amy said.

"I could go for a sub sandwich," Randy said.

Wes laughed. "Opinionated bunch, aren't you? Why don't

I pull off the freeway first, and then we can see what our options are."

Before Wes could exit, a red light on the control panel came on and flashed a warning. "That's strange," Wes said.

"Is something wrong?" Sierra asked.

"I'm not sure. Did this light go on while you were driving?"

"No. I've never seen it go on before."

A sudden hiss of steam began to spit from the van engine and rise up like a cloud in front of the windshield.

"Oh, boy," Wes muttered. "Everybody hold on. I may have to pull over quickly. Houston, we have a problem."

Sierra shot her brother a look that said, "How can you be trying to make jokes when we're about to blow up here on the freeway?"

Wes was able to reach the off-ramp by turning on the windshield wipers and spraying the window to keep it clear. A distinct odor of moldy socks began to permeate the van.

"Smells like the radiator hose," Randy said.

"You can tell what's wrong with a car by its smell?" Vicki asked.

"Sometimes. When you drive a truck as old as mine, you get used to these things happening all the time." Randy leaned forward and peered through the hazed-over windshield. "Is that an auto-parts store next to the gas station?"

"Where?" Wes said, driving slowly while the traffic zoomed past him. One driver honked at them and looked angry as he sped around the van.

"Over there, next to the Denny's. On the right."

"I see it."

Before Wes could put on his turn signal, a furious screeching sounded behind them. Sierra turned around and saw a huge truck barreling toward them, recklessly fast.

chapter nine

"H E'S GOING TO HIT US!" AMY SCREAMED.
Sierra grabbed the side of the seat, waiting for the crash. Wes stepped on the gas and swerved the van into the parking lot of the auto-parts store just as the truck driver blew his horn and rolled past them. He missed them by only inches.

"That was way too close," Vicki said, closing her eyes and putting her hand over her face.

"What was that guy doing?" Amy said.

"I wonder if he couldn't stop," Sierra said, trying to see the truck out the side window. She watched as it sped up to catch a yellow light. Then the road curved, and the truck kept on going until she couldn't see it anymore. "Bunch of maniac drivers in this town."

"The main thing I care about this town is that it has an auto-parts store that's open," Wes said, turning off the engine and getting out of the van. The rest of them followed him.

Billows of steam rolled from under the van's closed hood. The disgusting smell of moldy socks was even stronger outside.

"You're not going to open it, are you?" Amy asked. "It looks as if it's going to explode."

"I think you're right, Randy," Wes said. "It's probably a hose. I'll give it awhile to cool, and then we can check it out. Do you girls want to go eat something at Denny's?"

"Trying to get rid of us?" Amy teased. "You afraid we women might get in the way of your manly car repairing?"

"You can stay here, if you want. I was trying to be nice," Wes said.

"I was only kidding." Amy gave him a punch in the arm. Sierra tried to watch the interaction between them without appearing to stare.

"I'm ready to eat," Vicki said. "I'll save us a booth at Denny's. Anyone else want to come?"

Sierra joined her, and the two of them walked across the parking lot, leaving Amy, Wes, and Randy to deal with the car.

"Vicki, do you think Amy is showing extra interest in Wes?"

"I hadn't noticed," Vicki said. She held open the door of the restaurant for Sierra. "I don't think she's overdoing it or anything. She admires Wes. She always has. I don't think you should start to worry about anything being out of balance."

"Two?" the hostess asked, greeting them with menus in her hand.

"There will be five of us," Sierra said. "And we would like nonsmoking, please."

The waitress said, "This is all nonsmoking. All restaurants are nonsmoking in California." She led them to a large booth in the corner.

"I wish they had that rule in Oregon," Vicki said. "I can't stand it when you're trying to eat, and it tastes like ashes from the person's cigarette at the table five feet away."

Sierra was only half listening. From the corner window

she had a good view of the van. The hood was up, steam was pouring out, and another guy had joined Wes, Randy, and Amy in gazing into the abyss of the van's engine area. Sierra noticed that Amy was standing rather close to Wes and looking up at him as if she were hanging on to his every word.

"You really don't think Amy is going to make an effort to capture Wes's special attention this trip? I don't know if you remember, but it got a little complicated on our backpacking trip last summer. Her interest in him put a strain on our friendship. I don't want it to get like that on this trip." Sierra was still looking out the window as she spoke, so she couldn't see Vicki's expression.

"Do you know if they serve fish here?" Vicki said, scanning her menu. "I feel like having fish sticks or something."

"Fish sticks?" Sierra shook her head. Vicki hadn't heard a word she'd said. Or she had heard and was trying to get out of responding.

The waitress took their order and left glasses of ice water for them. Sierra turned again to watch the happenings beyond the window. Wes, Amy, and the other guy had gone into the auto-parts store, leaving Randy at the van with his hands plunged into its front end. She thought how nice it was to have Randy along, since he was experienced with car problems. Before Randy had suggested the problem might be a hose, Sierra had been worried something was seriously wrong with the van, and their trip would have to be canceled.

"You know," Sierra said when the waitress delivered Vicki's salad, "I'm glad Randy came, and I'm glad you invited him."

"He's glad you included him," Vicki said, picking over the lettuce and scraping most of the creamy dressing to the side of her small plate.

"You know what else?" Sierra said. "So far I haven't noticed your acting much different toward Randy."

"What do you mean?"

"You're the same person around him on this trip that you are at school and that you are when you're around Amy and me. I mean, I know you like him, and you would love for him to pay extra attention to you, but I don't see your going out of your way to . . ." Sierra couldn't find the right word.

"Flirt?" Vicki filled in for her. "The way I used to?"

"I wasn't going to use that exact word," Sierra said.

"No, it's true. I've given up flirting. If Randy is going to like me, he's going to like me for who I am and how I act 24–7."

"24–7?" Sierra questioned.

"You know, 24 hours a day, seven days a week. And, by the way, Amy isn't exactly flirting with your brother, if that's where you're headed with all this."

"I didn't say she was."

"Trust me. I know about flirting, and I know about Amy around guys she likes and wants to impress. She is being herself right now, and I don't think she is out of balance, or whatever you called it, at all."

The waitress arrived with Sierra's hamburger and Vicki's fish dinner. They prayed together quietly. Vicki's prayer and her earlier words made Sierra feel as if she were being a nosy, spiteful sister and friend. She didn't want to be like that. With all her might, Sierra tried to remember the verse about casting down her imagination. Only a few of the words came to her, but they were enough of a wakeup call to get her mind on other things—like the desserts advertised in the clear acrylic frame in the middle of the table.

"You want to split one of these desserts?" Sierra asked

Vicki, holding her burger with both hands and pointing at the picture with her little finger.

"You haven't even taken a bite of your dinner, and you're already planning dessert," Vicki said.

Sierra quickly took a bite and swallowed. "There. Now I've had a bite. Let's plan dessert."

Vicki laughed and agreed to split dessert with her.

Wes, Randy, and Amy joined them and slid into the booth before the dessert arrived.

"We're back on the road again," Wes said. "Thanks to Randy and that guy who came to help us."

Randy grinned his half grin and shrugged. "Like I said, knowledge comes from experience, and my truck provides me with plenty of experience."

Sierra gingerly reached for Randy's right hand and drew it up to the light. "And what does experience teach you about coming to the table with grimy hands?"

Wes automatically checked his own hands. The two young men sheepishly slid out of the booth and headed toward the rest room.

"You know," Amy said, "there's probably just as much bacteria on our hands, even though they're not covered with grease."

"Thank you for telling us after we've eaten," Sierra said.

"I ate with my fork," Vicki said, dipping her fork into the ice-cream-covered brownie she and Sierra were sharing.

"I'm going to get one of those," Amy said, slapping the menu closed and laying it on the table.

"That's all?" Sierra asked.

"And a bowl of soup. How's that for a balanced meal?"

"Who can worry about eating healthy on a trip like this?" Vicki said. "Or when we get to college, for that matter. My cousin said that when she went to college, she gained 10 pounds the first semester, and she spent more money on eating out than anything else."

Suddenly, Sierra realized that once she went to college in the fall, she was going to be on her own when it came to meals, or at least meals outside the cafeteria. She didn't like the idea of gaining 10 pounds her first semester. "We'll just have to all watch our diets and keep each other accountable," Sierra said. "Of course, I'm saying this as I stuff myself with this decadent dessert."

Wes and Randy returned and ordered their dinners while Sierra and Vicki finished up their dessert. The conversation swirled around, and Sierra participated in the fun. But a cloud of apprehension hung over her. The thought of going away to college suddenly was more serious than a lark of a road trip to California. Ahead of her lay more unknowns and more responsibility than she had ever experienced.

The uneasiness heightened when they returned to the van, and Wes said, "You want to drive for a while, Sierra? I'd like to go in the back and see if I can take a nap."

Sierra felt nervous. "Okay, I'll drive. Which way?"

"South," Wes said, handing her the keys with a smile. "I'll get you back on the freeway, then you just keep going south."

Randy climbed into the front passenger seat. "I'll be glad to drive, if you get too tired."

"Thanks, Randy. Just keep me awake, okay?"

Wes directed Sierra onto the freeway and then stretched out on the backseat. The traffic was light. The friends chatted, and Sierra kept checking the control panel on the dashboard to make sure no red lights came on.

"Does anyone have any idea where we are?" Sierra asked.

"Isn't there a map around here?" Randy felt beneath the

passenger seat. "Sunflower seeds," he said, holding up a bag that was circled by a thick rubber band.

"No thanks," Vicki said. "I'm trying to cut back on my natural foods this trip."

"Flashlight," Randy announced, pulling out the next item. "This may come in handy." He pulled out a map just as Sierra read the freeway sign they were speeding by. "Weed, next exit."

"Weed?" Vicki echoed with a laugh. "What kind of place is that?"

"I have no idea. Randy, check the map. Tell me I didn't take a wrong turn somewhere, and we're in the middle of Idaho."

"I don't think there is a Weed, Idaho."

"Just check the map."

Randy turned on the flashlight and searched the map. "Here it is," he announced finally. "Weed. It's definitely in California. You're doing fine, Sierra. We're in the right state."

Sierra wondered if Randy understood her anxiety and was trying to get her to laugh so she would relax. She gripped the wheel tightly, very much aware that she was once again in the driver's seat, and everyone was depending on her. Being responsible while plunging into the unknown was not something she was enjoying at all.

chapter ten

*A*S THEY DROVE ON INTO THE NIGHT, SIERRA FELT the tension building in her shoulders. It was getting foggy, and the flash of the oncoming headlights bothered her.

"According to the map," Randy said, "we're driving right past Mount Shasta about now. Did you realize the elevation of Mount Shasta is 14,162 feet?"

"You would never know it," Vicki said, leaning forward to peer out the front windshield along with Sierra and Randy. "It's totally overcast. Do you think it's going to rain?"

"I hope not," Sierra said. "I have my heart set on sunshine all the way this trip."

"You know," Randy said, "this is like following God."

Sierra and Vicki waited for an explanation. Randy's melancholy artist's temperament would cause him to be quiet for a long spell, and then, suddenly, some wild bit of wisdom would tumble from his mouth. It was as if he was always thinking, processing, and taking in information until a silent buzzer went off inside him and—bing!—he spilled out a nugget of truth.

"Here we are in the dark," Randy finally said, "with thick clouds over us, going full speed ahead, and right out there somewhere is this huge mountain, only we can't see it."

"And you think that's like God's will?" Vicki asked.

"Yeah. Because sometimes . . ." Randy paused as if for dramatic effect. ". . . we have to keep going on faith even when we can't see what's out there."

In Sierra's state of nervousness, she felt like telling Randy he was "out there" all right, but she kept her feisty thoughts to herself.

"Remember how God says His Word is like a lamp to our feet and a light to our path?" Randy continued. "Well, that's like now, when all we can see is a few yards ahead of us by the light of the high beams. We can't see the final destination or even some of the obvious markers along the way. The only thing we can see is what is right in front of us."

"That is so profound, Randy," Vicki said.

Sierra wasn't so sure it was profound, but then she didn't have a crush on Randy the way Vicki did. She wished Amy hadn't fallen asleep and was listening to this. Sierra thought Amy was the one who needed to understand God's will.

A raspy, guttural sound broke into their conversation, and Sierra said, "What did I tell you?"

"That's your brother?" Vicki asked. "Are you sure it isn't a broken muffler or something? I've never heard anyone snore like that."

"Get used to it. You'll be hearing a lot of that these next few days."

"This is how I see it," Randy said, ignoring Wes's snoring. "God's will, I mean." He pulled a straw out of the empty soda cup in the trash and held it up in the air. "This straw represents all of time as we know it, from beginning to end. We're limited to this because we're stuck on this straw. But God . . ." Randy cocked his head and gave Sierra a crooked smile. "God is completely outside of time. He's not limited to just this space of time as we are."

"You think God can see everything at once, so He knows what's going to happen before it even happens?" Vicki asked.

"Yes, that's what I believe," Randy said. "He is outside of the events and sequences. He isn't limited in any way, as we are. I think that at the exact same instant God went walking in the garden with Adam and Eve, He is also with us, right this second, driving down to Southern California."

Sierra felt a tiny shiver go up her spine. It was astounding to think of God being with them right now, just as He was present with Adam and Eve. Something deep inside of her began to calm down. *God, You really are right here, aren't You? You're in control.*

Vicki said, "So, you think God knew Warner was going to break his arm because He could see it happen ahead of time?"

"I think so," Randy said, tucking the straw back into the trash bag. "But I don't think God, like, sent an angel to slam on the brakes and make the accident happen. A lot of junk happens to us when we go our own way and don't even try to listen to God."

"You know what, Randy?" Vicki said. "You have to write a song about all this. Don't you think? This would make a great bunch of lyrics."

"Not a bad idea. Can you reach my guitar back there without waking up Wes?"

"I think so."

For the next two hours, Amy slept, Wes snored, Sierra drove, Randy strummed his guitar, and Vicki scribbled down every random phrase as Randy sang:

The high beam is all I have
to lead me down Your way.
Darkness hides Your wonders;
I beg for light of day.
Is Your face right there, behind that cloud?
I wanna know. I wanna see You.
Outside of time,
inside my mind,
it's You—always You.

"This is going to be an awesome song," Vicki said.

"It's a start," Randy answered and went back to strumming his guitar.

After all the anxiety Sierra had been feeling, Randy's soft strumming and coming up with song lyrics brought a calmness. The next few hours turned into the most peaceful time Sierra could remember experiencing—and the most astounding. She couldn't stop thinking about how God was right there with them.

When they needed to stop again for gas, they were close to Sacramento, and it was the dead of night. Yet Sierra didn't feel afraid.

Wes woke refreshed and thanked Sierra. He hadn't expected her to drive so far. When they hit the road again with Wesley at the wheel, Sierra was the one stretched out in what Vicki now called "the snore zone" on the backseat. Sierra slept soundly until they stopped somewhere in a busy parking lot. She opened her eyes and felt stiff all over. Raising her head, she looked out at what appeared to be her brother's reason for stopping.

"In and Out Burger!" Wes announced. "Everybody out."

Sierra yawned and tried to get her eyes to unstick at the corners of her lids. "What time is it?"

"It's time for a double double and a vanilla shake," Wes said.

This fast-food chain hadn't found its way to the Great Northwest, but Wes had made it known, when they first talked about going on the trip, that he planned to stop at every In and Out Burger they came upon. Apparently, this was the first one, which meant they had to officially be in the southern region of California, since that's the only part of the country where In and Out Burgers could be found.

Sierra knew by the brightness and warmth of the sun coming through the windows that they were well into the new day and that none of the clouds from the Mount Shasta area had followed them down here.

As the others scrambled from the van, eager for something to eat, Sierra fumbled for her backpack and, with another yawn, locked the van doors behind her. There was a line inside the restaurant. From the large menu over the register, it appeared that the place served only hamburgers, fries, shakes, and soft drinks.

"Do you want me to order for you?" Wes asked Sierra.

"Sure. I'm going to the rest room."

"What do you want?"

Sierra twisted her dry mouth into a grin and said, "Fish sticks."

"What?"

"Never mind. Surprise me."

Wes shook his head. Sierra didn't see Amy and Vicki in the food line, so she guessed they were already in the rest room.

"At least there's not a line for the bathroom," Sierra muttered as she pushed open the door and saw her friends standing in front of the long mirror.

"I look like road kill," Amy said flatly. "Look at my hair!"

Vicki wasn't moaning. Instead, she had gone to work, pulling a few necessities from her backpack: a toothbrush, washcloth, hairbrush, and makeup bag. She even had a clean T-shirt, which she quickly slipped over her head after she had washed her face and the front part of her hair.

"That's not fair," Amy said, examining Vicki after her three-minute freshening-up routine produced impressive results. "You can get gorgeous with just a sink and a squirt of hair spritz. I need a hot shower and a minimum of an hour."

"You guys want to borrow anything?" Vicki asked, holding out her stuffed backpack. Her complexion looked flawless, her eyes were bright and clear, and her silky, brown hair was pulled smoothly back with a clip. She even smelled sweet.

"Leave the whole bag," Sierra said.

"Yeah, and go tell the guys we'll be out in an hour," Amy added. "I could sure use a change of clothes about now. All my stuff is tied up on the top of the van. I doubt Wesley would want to undo everything for a clean T-shirt."

"I have another one you can wear," Vicki said. "It's at the very bottom. It's white."

"Only one?" Sierra asked disappointedly. Her jeans weren't bothering her, but the light-blue, short-sleeved shirt she had put on yesterday morning was a crumpled, less-than-fresh mess with dots of chocolate stains on it.

"Sorry. Only one," Vicki said. She brushed past a woman with two little girls who were entering the rest room in a hurry. "I'll tell the guys you'll be right out."

"Don't hold your breath," Amy said. She began to pull stuff from Vicki's backpack and hand it to Sierra. "This is hopeless, really. We'll never be able to pull off the same transformation trick Vicki just did."

"I'll settle for a clean face," Sierra said. "And does she have any large hair clips in there? It's hot here. I want to get my hair off my neck."

Amy and Sierra made a noble attempt at freshening up. They encouraged each other all the way, saying how much better the other now looked. Only, Amy's short, dark hair still bulged a little in the back, despite the way she doused it with warm water. And Sierra's eyes remained bloodshot— evidence that she had strained them during her stint as the midnight road warrior.

"I give up," Amy said.

She zipped shut Vicki's backpack, slung it over her shoulder, and exited with Sierra.

Wes, Randy, and Vicki waved at them from one of the tables in the far left corner of the small eating area. Before them were five cardboard tray boxes, all stuffed with burgers and fries. The drinks were in large white cups with red stripes around them.

Sierra examined one of the cups. "Are these little palm trees between the stripes? How cute!"

"How California!" Amy added, enjoying the discovery.

"Look on the inside rim on the bottom," Wes said.

All four of them lifted their cups and checked the underside, looking for a door prize.

"Hey!" Randy said, the first to find the treasure. "That's cool."

"It has John 3:16," Sierra said, looking closely at hers. "That is so cool."

"And did you see how fresh these are?" Randy asked, a handful of the thin, golden fries in his hand. "A guy is in the back shoving potatoes into a slicer and then dipping them in the fryer. You have to try these."

"We'd better hurry," Vicki said, grabbing a handful from the mound in front of them. "Before Randy eats them all."

They agreed, after they had stuffed themselves, that Wes was right about enjoying the full California experience by stopping at In and Out Burger. The only problem was they all groaned when they got back in the van and were sure that the seat belts wouldn't fit them anymore.

Sierra sat beside the window in the middle seat. Amy was next to her, Vicki was in the front, and Randy was happily stretched out in the snore zone. Within minutes they were back on the freeway with the windows open and the warm breezes swirling through the van.

"Mind if I try to find a good radio station?" Vicki asked.

"Wait a minute," Sierra said. "First I have a few questions for you, brother dear. Where are we? Where are we going, and how long before we get there?"

"We're south of Bakersfield. Our first stop is Valencia Hills Bible College, and we should be there in an hour or less, depending on how quickly we get over the Grapevine."

"Now I have a question," Amy said. "Will we have a chance to take a shower between now and then?"

Wes laughed.

"I'm serious," Amy said.

Wes glanced over at Vicki, and after looking her over quickly, he said, "Why? You guys look fine. Am I starting to smell or something?"

"No," Amy said, "but I think I am."

"You're fine," Wes said. "Besides, the idea is for you to check them out. No one will be checking you out."

"Oh, thanks a lot!" Amy said.

"No, I didn't mean it that way," Wes said, glancing at Amy

in the mirror. "I meant you look fine. You look good just the way you are, really."

Sierra tried to discern how Amy had taken Wes's comment. His words had brought a subtle smile to her lips.

A red light on Sierra's emotional control panel lit up as she thought, *Did my brother just flirt with Amy?*

chapter eleven

"**C**AN I TRY FINDING A RADIO STATION NOW?**" VICKI** asked.

"Go ahead and try," Wes said. "As soon as we start to climb the Grapevine, it'll be hard to find anything. You'll have more success once we drop down into the L.A. basin."

"Is that the Grapevine?" Sierra said, noticing that the wide highway ahead led into an impressive bank of hills. It appeared even more impressive because of the long, flat, straight stretch of freeway they were traveling on. Sierra looked out the back window and thought the valley behind them was beautiful in a desolate sort of way. It seemed strange to think that all the flat farmland they had raced past was about the last undeveloped area of western Southern California. She knew that once they drove over the Grapevine into the San Fernando Valley, it would basically be one long stretch of developed civilization all the way to the Mexican border.

"Can you hand me the map?" Sierra asked. "I want to figure out where we are." Locating the red line on the map that was marked as the 5 Freeway, Sierra said, "I don't know why they call it the Grapevine. It's a pretty straight-looking road."

"Maybe the original highway had more twists and turns," Wes suggested.

"We're going to drive through the Los Padres National Forest," Sierra remarked. "Fraiser Mountain on our right is 8,026 feet high, and Sawtooth on our left is more than 5,000 feet." Then, because she realized she sounded like a tour guide, she added, "And postcards will be available at the end of our tour."

"Are we going to Santa Barbara?" Amy asked.

"No," Wes said. "That's on the other side of the mountains on the coast."

"Drake was the one who wanted to go to Santa Barbara," Vicki said.

"That's right. So, where are the colleges located that we'll see?" Amy asked.

Sierra went over the list, and she and Amy tried to find the campuses on the map.

As the van climbed the steady incline of the Grapevine, Vicki searched for an agreeable sound on the radio. All she managed to come up with was a loud song in Spanish and lots of crackling static.

"I give up. Oh, you guys, look at the hills!"

Sierra looked up from the map and was amazed at the sight. As far as they could see, wild California poppies poured over the hillside, waving to them with their bright-orange petals raised high.

"It's beautiful," Sierra said.

Randy, who had been quiet back in the snore zone, perked up at the sight of the flowers. "Wow," he said appreciatively. "It looks as if some giant devoured a huge bag of cheese-flavored chips and then wiped his hands on the hills."

Sierra laughed. "You have such a way with words, Randy!"

"Yeah," Amy teased, "as long as those words have to do with food."

At the In and Out Burger, Randy had eaten half of Amy's hamburger because she couldn't finish it. He also had scarfed down everyone's leftover fries.

"We all find our inspiration in different forms." Having said that, Randy lay back down, quietly humming to himself.

He was still humming after they had toured the Valencia Hills Bible College campus. He gave Sierra the impression of an absentminded composer trying to get the melody just right for his new song.

The five of them were leaving the main part of the campus and returning to the parking lot when Sierra looked around one more time. She tried to picture herself going to school here. She decided she liked the campus. She liked the way the dorms were set up in suites with a common living-room area. She liked the friendly students. Two of them even said hello to Sierra and her friends. She also liked the warm weather and wished she were wearing shorts instead of jeans.

What Amy liked the most was the student adviser who took them on tour. "Noah," Amy repeated to Sierra as they walked ahead of the others back to the van. "Isn't that a great name. Noah. It's so strong. And did you see the tattoo on his thumb?"

"That was a birthmark," Sierra said.

"It was not."

"Then it was a weird tattoo because it was a big, brown splotch."

Amy shook her head. "It was a tattoo of a bear or something."

She tugged at the front passenger door of the van, forgetting it was locked and Wes had the key. As she jiggled the door, the car alarm went off. Amy shrieked and jumped back. Sierra turned to see if Wes was still behind them. All he had to do was push a button on the keypad, and even from a distance, this terrible racket would stop. But Wes was nowhere in sight. Neither was Vicki or Randy.

"Where did they go?" Amy shouted with her hands over her ears.

"I don't know. They were right behind us."

Two college guys in a red compact car slowed down in the parking lot and looked out the driver's window at Amy and Sierra. A collapsed windsurfing board and sail were strapped to the roof.

"You okay?" the driver asked.

He had short, bleached hair, a deep tan, and an engaging smile. From the look of the rippling muscle on his left arm when he stuck it out the window, he definitely knew how to use the equipment he was carrying.

Amy immediately dropped her hands away from her ears and went over to his car. "The alarm accidentally went off," she called out, leaning over to see the driver. "Wes has the keys. He should be here any minute."

Sierra was amazed at how Amy could start up a comfortable, friendly conversation with any guy anywhere.

"Wes Langerfield?" the guy asked.

"No, Wes Jensen. He doesn't go here."

"Oh," the guy shouted back. "You go here, don't you?"

"No."

Sierra watched as Amy smiled, and she wondered if her cute friend with the little bump of wayward hair on the back of her head would admit she was still in high school.

"Do you want a ride back to the main campus to find Wes?" the driver offered.

"Sure," Amy said.

"I think we'd better wait here." Sierra quickly stepped in.

The guy in the passenger seat leaned over and smiled at Sierra. He was definitely another trophy-winning, lifeguard type.

"Are you sure?" he asked.

"Yes, I—" Before Sierra could finish her sentence, the screeching alarm stopped. Sierra looked over her shoulder to see Wes jogging toward them, still pointing the alarm pad toward the van.

"That must be Wes," the driver said.

Amy smiled. She nodded.

Sierra smiled. She nodded.

They both stood there, smiling and nodding.

"We'll see you around," the driver said as he gave a wave and put his car in first gear. "Take it easy." And off they went.

"You big flirt," Sierra teased, giving Amy a swat on the arm.

"Flirt? *Moi?*" Amy's dark eyes twinkled. "You were a little taken yourself, if I'm not mistaken."

Sierra shared a giggle with her friend. "You have to admit, they were two gorgeous examples of God's creation, weren't they?"

Amy gave Sierra a perturbed look. Sierra guessed it was because she had brought God into the conversation. "Hey," Sierra said quickly, "I'm only giving glory where glory is due."

"What happened?" Vicki said, rushing up to join them. "Did someone try to break into the van? Here? At a Bible college?"

"No," Sierra said with a wry grin. "Amy was demonstrating to me some of her techniques for meeting men on a college campus. And I do emphasize the word *men!*"

"And my techniques seemed to work quite well," Amy added, sharing another laugh with Sierra.

"I missed something," Vicki said.

"And how!" Sierra said.

"All I know," Amy said as she climbed into the front passenger seat of the van, "is that we can turn around and go home now. I know where I'm going to college in September!"

Sierra laughed again. "September? I thought you would want to start this summer. I imagine they offer windsurfing during the summer. You do have a growing interest in that sport, don't you?"

Amy laughed even harder. "I do now!"

"What is with you two?" Wes said.

He got in and closed the door. Rather than put the keys in the ignition and drive off, he turned in his seat to face the group. Sierra slid in next to the window on the middle seat. It gave her a strange sense of comfort that Amy was talking so freely about the guys they had met in front of Wes. Or was that a subtle way of letting Wes know some guys had ended up "checking her out"?

"We need to make a choice now," Wes said.

"There is no choice," Amy said. "I get the driver!" Again she burst out laughing, and Sierra with her.

"I think sleep deprivation is catching up with us," Vicki said. "Amy is going to lose it in about two seconds. You watch. When she starts laughing really hard, she snorts."

"I do not!" Amy protested, pulling a straight face. Her shoulders shook slightly as she tried to contain her laughter.

"Yes, you do, Amy, and you know it," Sierra agreed.

Wes gave Amy a sympathetic look. "Don't feel bad. They accuse me of snoring."

"You do snore!" Amy said. "I heard you last night sawing logs back there in the snore zone."

"We all heard you, Wes," Sierra said.

"Well, can you all hear this? We need to make a decision. Now, you guys, listen."

Amy stifled her giggles.

"I told my friends we wouldn't be at their place until late tonight because I thought we were going to spend more time here on campus. But you all said you checked out everything you needed to."

Sierra nodded and noticed the others doing the same. It wasn't a very large campus, and none of them had any interest in sitting in on one of the doctrine classes, as Noah had suggested. The catalogs they had picked up would give the specific information on classes and registration. They were all ready to move on.

Wes checked his watch. "It's five after four now. We could do a couple of things. We could drive into Hollywood—"

"Yes!" Amy said.

"We would hit traffic all the way, and to be honest, Amy, I think you're going to be painfully disappointed with the real Hollywood once you see it. There's Grauman's Chinese Theatre with the handprints of the stars in cement, but aside from that, it's not much more than a crowded downtown strip of old buildings, junky souvenir shops, and lots of homeless people."

"When were you there?" Sierra asked.

"About a year ago when I came down with Ryan. Let me finish what I was saying. We can go on into L.A., as I said, or we can go a short way down the freeway to Magic Mountain." Wes ended his suggestion with a Cheshire cat grin, which meant the last suggestion was what he really wanted to do.

"Magic Mountain," Randy called out from the backseat.

"Amy has coupons," Vicki said.

"Sounds good to me," Sierra said.

Everyone looked at Amy.

"Am I going to be the only one who doesn't go on the roller coasters?" she asked.

"Yes!" they all answered in unison.

"Okay, fine. Let's go to Magic Mountain. I can feed my rejected soul excessive amounts of cotton candy and sit on a bench waiting for you."

"Or you can live a little and come with us," Randy said.

In a scramble of searching for coupons and checking the map for directions, Amy, Sierra, Vicki, and Randy plotted their course while Wes drove.

"You can't miss the off-ramp," Sierra said. "This guide-book says you take the Magic Mountain Parkway exit, and it's right there."

"We'll be able to see it from the freeway," Wes said.

"You know what? This is great because these coupons are only good on weekdays," Vicki said, examining Amy's contribution. "We couldn't use them if we came back on the weekend. This is going to be so much fun!"

Sierra agreed with Vicki. She had never been to Magic Mountain, and today she was definitely in the mood to go a little crazy and have some fun.

"I only wish I could have had a shower," Amy said. "It's so much hotter here than at home. Doesn't anyone else feel a little less than fresh?"

"Don't worry," Wes said. "There are rides here guaranteed to freshen you up even if you don't go on them."

"What is that supposed to mean?" Amy asked.

"I can't tell you. I'll have to show you," Wes said as he pulled into the huge parking lot. The lot wasn't completely full, which made Sierra think going late on a Thursday afternoon was a lot better than trying to go on Saturday.

"Is anyone else going to take a sweatshirt?" Sierra asked. She was warm now like Amy, but she knew it could get chilly once the sun went down.

"Not a bad idea," Wes agreed. "Once we're inside the park, I don't want to have to come all the way back out here."

Armed with money, sweatshirts, and Amy's discount coupons, the five friends headed for the park entrance, joking and laughing all the way.

chapter twelve

"**H**EY THERE! HOW'S EVERYBODY DOING? ARE ALL five of you together? How about if all of you stand right there, and I'll take your picture?" A young man wearing a park uniform held up a large camera. He and several others stood at the entrance to Six Flags Magic Mountain Amusement Park offering to capture the entrants on film.

"Sure," Vicki answered for them. She struck a pose with her arm resting on Randy's shoulder.

Sierra caught Randy's expression under the bill of his baseball cap. He looked surprised that Vicki was leaning on him. Surprised, but kind of enjoying it.

Sierra looped her arm through Wes's, and Amy did the same with his other arm. Vicki moved closer to Amy and wrapped her other arm around Amy's neck.

"Terrific," the photographer said, quickly capturing the shot while they held their chummy pose. "Here's a ticket for you. If you would like to buy a copy of your photo, you can turn this into the photo station and pick up the picture when you leave the park."

"I definitely want a copy," Vicki said.

"So do I," said Sierra.

"Me, too," Amy said.

The three girls looked at Randy.

"Whatever," he said with a shrug.

"I'll visit your picture, Sierra, whenever I need a memory," Wes said, leading them to the photo station.

His comment made Sierra realize how great he had been about this whole trip. Wes was so much older than the rest of them, yet he never treated them as if they were beneath him. If there was an award for the best big brother, Sierra would have nominated Wesley.

"Where to first?" Vicki asked after they had turned in their orders for the picture.

"Anybody else ready for the Viper?" Wes said.

"What's that?" Amy asked, sticking close to his side.

They walked past a large, circular water fountain. Sierra felt a delicate mist as the late afternoon breeze caught the fountain spray and taunted her with its refreshing coolness.

"I could go for something to drink," Sierra said.

"What about the Tidal Wave?" Randy asked. "That one sounded pretty good from what the guidebook said."

"Yes," Wes said with a grin, "this might be a nice time of day to visit the Tidal Wave."

"Just point me to the gift shops and food court," Amy said. "That's where I'll be waiting for you guys."

"Oh, come on," Sierra said. "Don't be like that. You would like lots of the rides here. I'll go on them with you. And who knows? You might just feel brave enough to try one of the really fun rides."

"Don't get your hopes up," Amy said. She wasn't wearing the expression of someone who was rebelliously enduring this trip. She merely looked uncomfortable—as though she would just like to have a shower and a nice, clean bed to crawl into.

Sierra had to admit she had seen Amy's hair look better. And the dark shadows under her eyes appeared to be more from fatigue than smeared makeup. Amy was definitely one of those people who did better with a bath and a blow dryer than she did with going creatively au naturel, like Vicki and Sierra.

As a matter of fact, Sierra wouldn't have minded a clean shirt before they attacked the amusement park. A hot shower would have been nice, too, but she could wait. They were here, and it was time to have fun.

Wes walked briskly through the stream of people, and the rest of them followed. He was obviously a man on a mission. They gave up trying to offer their suggestions of where to go and trotted after their trailblazer in the green knit shirt.

"This way," Wes called to them over his shoulder as he headed for a bridge. The sound of people screaming with delight grew louder as they followed Wes onto the bridge. "Hurry! This way, you guys," he called out, looking at them and then looking at the waterway that ran under the bridge.

"Right here, Amy," Wes said, putting his hands on her shoulders and standing behind her. She came up to about the middle of his chest, and as he held her in place with a pesky grin on his face, Amy turned to look up at him with a smile of admiration—apparently for his gentle gesture of holding her shoulders as they gazed at the elaborately decorated canal.

Sierra realized she had lost one of her earrings. Looking around on the ground and retracing her steps, she tried to see where the dangly silver earring had landed. People were tromping all around her, and she figured retrieving the lost jewelry was probably hopeless.

Looking up at her friends, she noticed Wes giving Randy a nod. As Sierra watched, Randy followed Wes's example and stood behind Vicki with his hands on her shoulders. Vicki's grin lit up her whole face. Like Amy, Vicki turned to give Randy a sweet look of affection.

Then it happened. A speeding boat loaded with screaming people came barreling down the shoot. On cue, Randy and Wes both ducked behind Vicki and Amy while holding the girls firmly in place. The huge spray of water from the careening boat rose into the air and crashed down on them. Amy and Vicki were drenched—soaked to the skin. Amy's hair was completely flat and dripping water down her face. Randy and Wes looked well doused, too.

Vicki laughed. She laughed hard and beat Randy's chest with her fists as well as shook her wet hair on him. Sierra laughed, too, giving up on her earring and joining all her wet friends. She unfastened her remaining earring and tucked it into her pocket.

"I promised you a little freshening up, didn't I?" Wes teased Amy.

Amy didn't respond as Vicki had. Instead, Amy stood there, dripping, stunned, and looking as if she might cry. She turned her chin up toward Wes, pulled her soaked bangs from her eyes and said, "I can't believe you did that to me."

"Believe it," Wes said, still sporting his mischievous grin. "And unless you want to get it again, we'd better move off this bridge."

A chorus of screaming passengers announced the next boat was heading their way. The group scrambled off the bridge.

"You guys will be sorry," Vicki said, grabbing Amy by the wrist, "because now we're going to the rest room, and you'll have to wait for us. No telling how long it will be before we come out."

"No problem," Wes said. "You can find Randy and me in front of the funnel-cake stand. You see it over there?"

Vicki nodded and ducked into the rest room with Amy.

Sierra watched as Amy and Vicki disappeared into the rest room and Wes and Randy marched off to the food cart, slapping each other on the back. She had been afraid this would happen; she was the leftover.

Dozens of happy amusement park visitors streamed past her as she stood there. Sierra felt the same way she had when she was six and became separated from her family in a crowd at a concert they had attended one night. She had been taught as a child that if she ever got lost, she should stand still and wait. She had been promised an adult would come find her. This time, no one was coming to look for her.

At the concert, she had stood alone only a few minutes before her father's concerned face appeared in the crowd and his steady hand reached out and grasped hers. It was a vivid memory. The sudden rush of terror over being lost and alone had been replaced instantly with an overpowering sense of comfort and security when her father reached out for her. At the touch of his hand, Sierra had held on tight. She never wanted to feel that kind of loneliness and fear again.

Yet, here she was, 17 years old, doing exactly what she wanted to do, with all the people she wanted to be with, and fear had found her. Isolation circled her. It was as if she were six years old all over again. Only this time, no one was going to reach out his hand to grasp hers. Her father was 1,000 miles away.

Then a thought came to Sierra, the kind of thought that starts in the heart and warms the spirit all the way through. Her heavenly Father was not 1,000 miles away. He was here with her—right beside her. He always was, and He promised He always would be.

That realization covered her with peace. Terror and all its icy companions fled. She felt as if God had invisibly slipped His nail-scarred hand into hers, and all she had to do was hold on tight.

"You are so real," she whispered into the unseen realm. "You're right here. I know You are. And You're never going to leave me, are You?" The calmness of the presence of God's Spirit in the middle of that busy crowd amazed Sierra.

She blinked and looked around, almost expecting people to stare at her, as though her hair were on fire or something. That's how changed she felt. But no one was staring. Apparently, no one else had sensed God's presence the way she had. He had done that just for her. With her heart full to the brim, Sierra headed for the rest room. She felt changed. She wasn't a little girl anymore. She didn't feel cut off from her friends or lost. She was loved, and she knew it.

Amy and Vicki were at work in front of the mirror, using all the beauty supplies Vicki had brought with her. Amy had combed her wet hair straight back and was standing in front of the heat-blasting hand dryer. Neither of them seemed to have noticed Sierra hadn't been with them all along.

The girls ended up spending less than 10 minutes in the rest room. Amy's shock over the dousing wore off, and a playful attitude took its place. When they met up with the guys, there was lots of joking, teasing, and even a little funnel-cake smashing into Randy's face.

Sierra wanted to tell everyone she had just had this amazing experience in which she understood God's presence as never before. But she found it awfully hard to have a serious conversation with someone who was holding a chunk of cake at the end of a plastic fork, ready to catapult it at her face.

"More cake, anyone?" Randy asked.

"None for me," Wes said, getting up. "I think I hear the Viper calling my name."

"Oh, yes, I can hear it," Vicki said. She made her best snake face and hissed out, "Wesssss-ley. Come to me, Wesssss-ley."

"Is that a roller coaster?" Amy asked reluctantly.

"Yes," Wes said, "it's a roller coaster."

"And does it go . . . ?" Amy made circles in the air with her finger.

"Only twice," Wes said. "It's over before you know what bit you."

Amy gave Sierra a pleading look. "Are you sure you want to go on it, Sierra?"

Sierra nodded. "Come on, Amy. You can always close your eyes."

"No way," Randy said. "You're not allowed to close your eyes. If you close your eyes, they stop the ride, and you have to get out and walk down the emergency stairs."

"What if you close your eyes when it's upside down?"

"They still make you get out," Randy said. "There's a safety net, so, you know, you just unhook your seat belt and down you go."

"You guys are mean," Amy said.

They were walking at a faster pace now. Wes was, once again, eager to reach his goal.

"Can't you accept that some people have a death wish and some people don't?" Amy kept talking louder. "I mean, why should this be a test of my tolerance for fear? Can't you see that in this life there are rollers and nonrollers? I'm in the minority here because I'm a nonroller. So what? Isn't it time we all started honoring diversity?"

By the time Amy finished her speech, Wes had led them to the end of the line for the Viper. After ushering Sierra, Vicki, and Randy into line, he hung back with Amy.

"You guys go ahead," he said.

The line was moving quickly. Two other guys immediately got in line behind them, making it impossible for Wes to slip in with the three of them.

As the crowd pressed forward within the railings, Sierra looked over her shoulder and was surprised at what she saw. Wes was bent slightly, looking Amy in the eyes. Then he reached over and put his arm around her.

chapter thirteen

*T*HE LINE FOR THE VIPER MOVED SO QUICKLY SIERRA soon couldn't see what was going on with Amy and Wes. Was he counseling her as a big brother? Had she started to cry, and was he trying to comfort her? Or was he expressing affection for her?

Why does this bother me so much? she thought. *I'm all in favor of Vicki and Randy's getting together; so what's the big deal with Wes and Amy's getting together? Is it that I think Wes is too old for Amy?*

Sierra thought Wes couldn't be interested in Amy because he had certain criteria for what he was looking for in a girlfriend, and Amy didn't match that description. His first priority was that the woman must be a strong Christian. Amy had admitted more than once that she wouldn't necessarily put herself in that category. So, why was Sierra still nervous about any attention Wes gave Amy?

Vicki and Randy talked about the roller coaster as they inched toward the front of the line. They could see the loops and hear the screams of those who had gone before them. Vicki said she didn't like the way the structure made a clanging, rattling sound as the cars climbed the steep incline to the top of the first loop. Sierra nodded agreement but only half listened as she continued to process her thoughts about Wes and Amy.

By the time she reached the front of the line, Sierra figured out what was bothering her. She didn't want to share Wes with another girl. He was her big brother, and if he became attached to someone else, it would change everything.

Instead of freeing her, the realization made Sierra feel heavy. She knew she couldn't control her brother's life, and the only area she had any influence on Amy was in selecting clothes. This was something she had to let go of or it would hurt her relationships with Wes and Amy.

What's going on, God? Sierra prayed. *Two big revelations for me right in a row. First hold on, then let go. . . . What is this?*

The uniformed ride attendant on the platform motioned for Randy to climb into an open, single seat in a roller-coaster car. Sierra and Vicki were directed to the front seats in the first car.

"Front-row seats! What did we do to deserve this?" Vicki said, grabbing Sierra's arm as she stepped into the hard plastic car. "Is it too late to change my mind?"

They sat down, and the safety bar came down over their shoulders, locking them in. It was hard to move and impossible to say anything to Randy, who was several seats behind them.

"Yes, I think it's too late to change your mind," Sierra said. As the car lurched forward with a rocking motion, her stomach did a flip-flop. "Don't worry. You're going to love this. It'll be great!" she told Vicki.

"Are you sure?" Vicki asked in a nervous, high-pitched voice.

The car made its creaky, clanking climb to the top of the

rise. With their faces toward the sky, Sierra noticed how pale blue it was. To the right, an airplane left a white, dusty streak across the wide expanse of heaven. It might as well have been accompanied by the sound of fingernails on a chalkboard because that sound gave her the same sensation she was feeling in her stomach as they neared the crest of the Viper's first loop.

"You know, you might be right," Sierra yelled over to Vicki. "I think I want off now."

"Sierra," Vicki shouted, pressing her leg against Sierra's in a show of moral support, "you're supposed to be the brave one here!"

Sierra pressed Vicki's leg back. They were at the top. Before them lay nothing but air. Sierra gripped the guard bar and let out a scream as the green nemesis plunged them into the depths of its belly. The rush of air pulled their hair straight back and drew the skin on their faces away from their wide-open mouths. In a matter of seconds, they were dropped, spun through two great loops, and spit out of the control booth with a jerk. Sierra and Vicki screamed the whole way.

Dazed, dizzied, and hoarse, they stumbled out of the car and waited for Randy. Randy's only evidence of the adrenaline rush was his crooked grin.

"Ready to go again?" he asked.

"I don't think so," Vicki said, gripping her sides.

"That was great!" Sierra said, her voice loud and raspy. "Wes is going to love this one! Where do you guys think he is?"

They exited together, awkwardly bumping into each other and apologizing with their shared laughter. Wes and Amy stood a few feet from the exit.

"You're going to love it!" Sierra announced when she spotted her brother.

"I'm ready," Wes said. "Who else is game?"

"I am," Randy said.

"Not me," Vicki said with a moan. "Why did I eat all that cake?"

"I found a ride that's more my speed," Amy said. "Anyone want to go on a kiddy ride with me?"

"I'll go with you," Vicki said.

Sierra debated before deciding to go with Vicki and Amy. "Where should we meet you guys?"

Wes pointed out a spot for them to meet, and they agreed to be there in about 40 minutes.

"Are you okay, Amy?" Vicki asked as they leisurely went in search of the Gold Rush, Amy's ride.

"Yes. I'm sorry if I was being a drag on everyone."

"I didn't think you were," Vicki said.

"Well, Wes was worried, I guess."

"Did you two have a good talk?" Sierra asked.

"Yes, your brother is a true hero, Sierra. You know that, don't you? Of course you do. Wes has a way of making me think without feeling like a fool. I wish I still had a crush on him."

"You don't?" Sierra asked.

"No. Why? Have I been acting like I do?"

"Not really. Maybe a little." Sierra noticed the sign above the entrance to the Gold Rush as they were about to walk past it. "Here it is, you guys. And the line is even short."

Not only was the line short, but so were most of the people in it. Everyone seemed to be less than 10 years old, except for the parents who accompanied their kids.

"There's not a height or weight limit on this, is there?" Vicki asked.

"No, I don't think so. I think it's a slow roller coaster," Amy answered.

"Not that either of you two have to worry," Vicki added.

"Are you saying we look like fifth-graders?" Amy asked.

"No, I'm saying the two of you together weigh about as much as I do by myself."

"Yeah, right," Amy said.

"Not even close," Sierra echoed. "Why do you say that?"

"Because I do weigh more than either of you."

"So? You're not too heavy or anything. You're fine. You're you. You're just right whatever size you are," Amy said. "Beauty has nothing to do with size."

"I know, I know," Vicki said. "I don't want to get into that discussion."

Sierra agreed; she wanted to discuss why Amy no longer had a crush on Wes. "So tell us what Wes said that made you feel better."

"We talked about my fear of roller coasters and heights, and Wes said he understood and wouldn't pressure me any-more. He asked if I was really upset about the water, and I told him it bothered me at first, but I got over it. I guess that's how I am about a lot of things." She shrugged her shoulders. "That was all. He was being a nice big brother to me, and I enjoyed every minute of it."

They climbed into the gold-colored cart, and Sierra scolded herself for being judgmental and suspicious of Amy. Sierra's imagination had taken off. She realized that if she had been so incorrect in her assessment of what was going on with Amy and Wes, she might be misjudging other things as well. If she was so out of balance, was it really a good idea to try to make this huge, life-changing decision about where she would go to college?

The panicked feelings returned. It didn't matter that a short while ago she had felt God beside her, holding her hand. Right now her emotional roller coaster was going through a big loop, and she felt overwhelmed with all the unknowns that lay in her future.

"Now that was a thriller," Vicki teased when they exited the tame roller-coaster ride. It was designed to resemble a mining cart traveling through a gold mine.

Sierra didn't think it would win any awards either—especially not after the Viper.

"Hey, I liked it. It was just my speed," Amy said. "So don't be mean."

They arrived at the meeting spot. Wes and Randy were already there and had planned out their next three wild rides: Batman, Superman the Ride, and Free Fall. Sierra and Vicki were all set to join them, but then they remembered Amy.

"It's okay, really," Amy said. "I don't mind going with you and waiting. These rides only take a few minutes once you get to the front of the line."

"Are you sure it's okay?" Sierra asked.

Amy shot an appreciative glance at Wes. "I'm sure."

Somehow Sierra found it hard to believe Amy no longer had a crush on him. But there was no time to evaluate the situation as the five of them tromped off to experience the thrills, chills, and spills of the Batman roller-coaster ride. Besides, Sierra's evaluation tank was already full with her anxieties over her future.

As they stood in line, the elaborately decorated Bat Cave loomed before them: dark, mysterious, and promising thrills.

Sierra couldn't help but equate it with her future and her decisions about college.

"What if we don't go away to college?" she suddenly said to Vicki.

"Where did that come from?" Vicki asked.

"I was thinking. What if we stay in Portland and go to a community college or even one of the universities but live at home?"

Vicki gave Sierra a look that asked if she had suddenly gone crazy. "What are you talking about? All you've been raving about for months is going away to school. You're our world-traveling role model, Sierra. You can't wimp out on us now."

Sierra gave Amy a wistful glance over her shoulder as they moved to the front of the roller-coaster line. Amy was sitting contentedly on a bench in the shade, sipping a cold soft drink. "There's something to be said for sitting this one out," Sierra said.

"What are you saying?" Vicki asked. "Sitting out your first year of college or sitting out this ride?"

Wes slipped his arm around Sierra's shoulders and gave her a squeeze. "Sounds as though you just discovered the real world, my little dreamer girl. It's about time. I hate to be the one to tell you this, but ignoring the future won't make it go away. Time to grow up, baby sis."

Sierra felt her cheeks turning red. Amy might idolize Wes for his counseling techniques, but at this moment his words brought Sierra only humiliation. If they hadn't been in such a public place, she would have slugged him in the stomach.

chapter fourteen

"**T**HAT WAS BY FAR THE MOST FUN I'VE EVER HAD at any amusement park anywhere," Sierra said. She settled into the front seat of the van as they drove out of the Magic Mountain parking lot. Her conflict with Wes had dissipated after they went on the Batman ride and after she decided to force her frustration and insecurities out of her mind to fully enjoy the rest of the time in the park.

"And this is by far the best souvenir I've ever gotten," Vicki added from the backseat, where she sat next to Randy. She held what looked like a toy telescope up to her eye. The telescope was also a key chain, and the photo taken of the five of them when they entered the park was at the end of the tube.

"I know," Amy agreed, holding up her key-chain souvenir. "I like this silly little thing, too. In case I haven't said this yet, Sierra and Wes, thanks so much for inviting me along. I'm having such a great time, I don't want to go home."

"We have a couple more days," Wes said. "That might be long enough for you to change your mind."

"I don't think so," Amy said. "I wish this trip was for a month. No, two months. Or all summer. That would be so cool. A whole summer on the road with your friends."

"As long as everyone who goes is friends with everyone else," Vicki said.

Sierra knew they were all thinking of what a different experience this would have been if Warner had ended up coming with them. No one said anything, though.

"I called Brad and Alissa while you guys were on that last ride. They said it would take us about an hour to get to their place," Wes said.

"What time do we have to be up in the morning?" Sierra asked.

"I'd like to leave Brad and Alissa's around 8:00."

Sierra groaned. "That early? Don't you want to spend more time with your friends?"

"Yeah, while we sleep in?" Amy added.

"They have a beach trip planned for tomorrow, so they're going to get an early start, too."

"The beach sounds like fun," Amy said. "By any chance are we going anywhere near the ocean?"

"We might later tomorrow," Wes said. "The main thing is that I have an appointment at Rancho Corona at 11:30. After that we can do whatever we want. I need to call Tawni to see if she's still expecting us at her place tomorrow night. She lives about two miles from the beach."

"You're kidding," Amy said. "I never realized that."

"I'm beginning to like Southern California more and more," Sierra said, stretching her arms over her head. "I can't imagine what it would be like to live near the beach." She reached for the side lever and reclined her seat halfway.

"Is the college you want to go to near the beach, Wes?" Vicki asked.

"I think Rancho Corona is about 20 or 30 miles inland from the coast. It's located on top of a mesa. They say on clear days you can see the ocean, and at sunset you can often see Catalina Island."

"What's a mesa?" Amy asked.

"It's a high, flat plateau."

"Doesn't *mesa* mean 'table' in Spanish?" Sierra asked.

"I think so. That would make sense. That's what it looks like. A big, flat tabletop."

Sierra closed her eyes and tried to imagine a college campus built on a mesa with a view of the sun setting into the Pacific. The thought brought a smile to her face and romantic images of a bright, shining citadel, a brave fortress filled with God-lovers. Even though she knew nothing about this college nor had seen any pictures of it, she liked it already.

And she liked it even more the next morning at 10:45, when the van turned off the freeway south of Lake Elsinore. Ahead of them stood a vast range of hills, including the mesa Wes had talked about. It was easy to spot because it was one of the highest places along the range and was perfectly flat all the way across the top. Above the plateau rose endless miles of clear sky marred only by a few lazy puffs of ragged clouds.

Sierra sat up straighter and peered through the front windshield. Wildflowers dotted the hillsides. She felt a sense of anticipation. Something about this area reminded her of Switzerland when she had visited last summer with her friend Christy. They had hiked among the cows and wildflowers in the deep green hills. Here, the terrain was a smear of warm terra-cotta and sandy-brown tones. Instead of lumbering cows with bells around their necks, as they had seen in Switzerland, Sierra imagined wild rabbits darting across the hiking trails.

" 'Rancho Corona University.' " Sierra read the sign at the

side of the road. " 'Turn right.' "

Wes turned right and headed up the road that led to the top of the mesa.

"This is a wonderful place," Sierra said dreamily.

"We're not there yet," Wes muttered. He sounded tired.

They were all tired—tired and grouchy after sleeping only five and a half hours on the floor before Wes woke them that morning. Amy had been insistent about a shower before they started the new day, and they all agreed it was a good idea for them, too. Brad and Alissa's duplex had only one bathroom, so that meant a long line.

Sierra's shower provided only cold water by the time it was her turn. She complained about it, but then felt bad later. It wasn't a very grateful attitude to show their hosts, especially since Brad had whipped up fried eggs, sliced ham, and buttery muffins for all of them, even though Wes had insisted they could buy breakfast on the road. She didn't feel any of those cranky emotions now.

"Are we supposed to meet with a counselor?" Amy asked. "I mean, can we just look around and wait for you, or do we have to talk to someone?"

"I set up a tour of the campus with one of their student volunteers, like at Valencia Hills," Wes said. "You guys can do whatever you want after you take the tour. I'll need at least three or four hours here."

The wide, steep road led to the top and then curved to the left. Two tall pillars of smooth rock stood at the campus's impressive entrance. A large, wooden sign arched over the entryway bearing the words, "Rancho Corona University." They followed the signs to the admissions office and parked in one of the spaces marked "Visitor."

"This doesn't look much like a college," Amy said. "It

looks more like a camp or a resort or something. I love all the tile roofs. It's like a set for an old Zorro movie."

"That's the early California look. I think this land used to be a ranch," Wes said. "We'll have to ask the tour guide. Is everybody ready? I'll leave the keys with you, Sierra, in case we go in separate directions and you guys want to come back to the van for anything."

"Somebody better wake up Randy," Vicki said, pulling back her hair and leaning forward from the rear seat to get out. Randy sat with his head against the window and his baseball cap pulled down over his face.

Amy turned around and reached over to remove the baseball cap. "Wake up, Randy. We're here."

He scrunched up his face at the sudden light and uncrossed his arms. With the back of his hand, he wiped the side of his mouth. Sierra had to smile. He looked like such a kid. She missed the way Randy looked when she had first met him and his long, blond hair hung straight down from a middle part. He used to tuck it behind his ears all the time. For months now he had worn it short so that at moments like this it tended to stick out and give him the appearance of Dennis the Menace.

Sierra was eager to have a look around. The grounds were beautiful. Magenta-colored bougainvillea vines climbed up the side of the admissions building and onto the red tile roof. She followed Wes into the building as the other stragglers got out of the van. The coolness of the air conditioned building breathed a welcome. The receptionist, a college-age student, sat behind a modern, oval desk and wore a phone headset.

She looked up at them, and her face beamed with an overly eager smile, almost as if she recognized them. "Are you Wesley Jensen?" she asked.

"Yes, I scheduled an appointment for 11:30."

"We've been expecting you. And you have to be Sierra," she said. Still beaming, she rose and shook their hands excitedly. "I'm so glad you both are here. Welcome to Rancho Corona!"

Sierra glanced at her brother. This welcome was a little overdone.

"There's someone who's been waiting to see you," the receptionist said. "Let me call her."

The receptionist was about to press one of the buttons on the panel before her when the front door opened and an exuberant female voice called out, "Are they here yet?"

Before Sierra could turn around, she heard a wild and vaguely familiar squeal. She felt the tackle of arms around her and a crushing hug and heard more wild laughter in her ear. The only clue she had as to who was welcoming her so enthusiastically came from a flash of red hair that had swished across her face like an oriental fan. But that one clue was all she needed.

chapter fifteen

"KATIE!" SIERRA NOW JOINED IN THE SQUEALS OF surprise as she pulled back to see her friend from arm's length. "Oh, I can't believe this! Katie, what are you doing here?"

The green-eyed, red-haired fireball blurted out the whole story in one long breath. "I go to school here, you goof! You never figured that out, did you? You e-mailed Christy last week and told her all about your trip down here so your brother could check out Rancho. . . . Hey, you must be Wes. Hi, I'm Katie. So I had my roommate here, Dawn, check out the visitors roster, and there you are. Dawn, this is Wes and Sierra. Wes and Sierra, this is Dawn. And she told me you were scheduled for today, so like the sneak I am, I didn't e-mail you to remind you that I went here because I wanted to surprise you, and I did! Is this a total God-thing or what?"

Sierra was laughing so hard at the way Katie's face turned red when she rattled on that Sierra hadn't noticed Amy, Randy, and Vicki entering the building and standing to the side, observing the event.

"Is this our campus tour guide?" Vicki asked.

Katie spun around, swishing her shoulder-length red hair as she turned. "That's me! I volunteered just for you guys.

Hi, I'm Katie. Sierra probably never told you anything about me. We only went to England and Ireland together last year."

"Oh," Amy said, stepping closer for a better look. "Did you say you're Christy?"

Katie threw up her arms and gave her audience a wild-eyed look with a bob of her head. "See what I mean? I'm the *other* one: Katie. Christy is the one everyone remembers. The one everyone talks about. The one everyone . . ." She paused to give Sierra a squinted glare. ". . . sends e-mails to. And me? I'm just Katie. Everybody's friend. Nobody's Friday night date."

Now they were all laughing, even Dawn, who was supposed to be answering the phone. They quieted down enough for introductions to be made all around and for Sierra to get over some of the shock of being greeted by her friend.

"I'd better lead us out of this area before I get us all in trouble," Katie said. "So let the tour begin. This is the admin building. The business offices are down that way, and, Wes, you get to meet with Mr. Scofield in that second office on the right, but not for another 20 minutes, so you might as well enjoy the tour."

Wes seemed captivated by Katie's quick wit and simple charm. He smiled one of his best smiles and said, "Lead the way."

Katie led them out the front door and past some more office buildings into a large central area. A blue-tiled fountain stood in the center of the plaza, and wrought-iron park benches circled the area. To the left, several tall palm trees rustled their long, elegant fronds high overhead. Their tree music gave the setting a balmy, tropical feeling. Several students sat on the edge of the fountain with their bare feet dangling in the water. Others stretched out on the benches in the shade, reading, sleeping, and talking.

"This is the Fountain Plaza and my favorite spot on campus. The long, two-story building on the right is the library; next to it is the Hannan Building. That's where all the English and language classes are taught. Behind it is the science building. And over here, on our far left, is Dishner Hall, which is the music building."

"I definitely want to check that one out," Randy said.

"No problem. We can see them all, if you want. But first, you need to see the Student Center."

The Student Center was located behind Dishner Hall and to the right. Katie hurried them through the two-story building, pointing out the mailboxes and Espresso Stop on the lower level before taking them upstairs to the open lounge area that led to an outdoor deck. From the deck they could view the swimming pool, track, gym, and baseball diamond.

"The ocean is out that way," Katie said, pointing to the right. "It's all smogged out today, but sometimes we can actually see it. Usually in the very early morning or at sunset."

Sierra lingered a little longer on the deck, imagining how the view would look once the pale yellow petticoats of smog were lifted from the sky's blue gown. It was a sight she wanted to see one day.

"Come on, Sierra," Katie said, motioning from the grass area below the deck where she now stood with the rest of the group. "We have a few more places to see before we send Wes back to admin."

"I'm coming." So much was hitting Sierra so quickly she wasn't sure she could take it all in. The university grounds held enough dreamy beauty by themselves. Being led around by Katie only added to the sensation that Sierra was imagining all this.

The cafeteria was the newest building on campus and was designed more like a mall food court than a typical school cafeteria.

"You should have seen the old cafeteria," Katie said as she shooed them back toward the administration building. "They said it was like an army mess hall. I never ate in it. I arrived here four days after the 'Sacred Caf' was completed, and I have nothing but stellar reports about the food."

"When did you start here?" Sierra asked.

"January. I transferred in from the community college at the beginning of the semester." Katie leaned closer to Sierra. "I've only been here three months, so don't feel bad about not knowing that. I don't think I even told you. I just wanted to give you a hard time."

Sierra looped her arm around Katie's neck and gave her a squeeze. "It's so good to see you. You'll have to tell me everything. I want to hear about everybody."

Katie flashed a sly grin at Sierra. "That can be arranged. I thought we would escort your brother to his appointment, go back to the Sacred Caf for some lunch, and talk our heads off."

"Do you guys want me to meet up with you some place later?" Wes asked. He stood at the door of the administration building, appearing a little hesitant to leave the rest of them.

"After we eat, I was going to take them down to the dorms," Katie said. "When your meeting is over, ask Dawn to call my room. How does that sound?"

"Good. I'll see you guys." Sierra noticed that Wes was running his fingers through the sides of his wavy, brown hair and looking a little nervous, as if he were going for a job interview.

Katie ushered them all back to the cafeteria and made

sure they took full advantage of the variety of food available by using their visitors' complimentary meal passes. Sierra barely paid attention to her salad, turkey sandwich, and glass of milk. Rather, she drank in and ate up every word Katie shared across the table.

According to Katie, this was an awesome school, and she planned to stay here until she graduated. Some of Katie and Christy's friends, whom Sierra had met last summer when she came to California for Doug and Tracy's wedding, also attended this school. Sierra's imagination filled with dreams of how wonderful it would be to go to college with these very special friends, especially if Wes was going to attend the graduate school here. Lost in her daydream, Sierra didn't hear Amy when she first spoke to her.

"Would that be okay with you?" Amy repeated, giving Sierra a nudge.

"What?"

"Vicki and I are going exploring. Randy went back for seconds, and you obviously are involved with your friend."

Sierra caught an edge of hurt in Amy's voice. It wasn't that Sierra meant to snub Vicki and Amy. It was just that this was Katie. In all the world there was only one Katie. They should understand that.

"Are you interested in seeing the dorms?" Katie asked as Amy rose to leave the table.

"Maybe a little later," Amy said.

"We'll be at the pool if you come looking for us," Vicki said. "I want to see if that California sunshine can do anything about this fish-belly white skin of mine." Vicki pulled up the sleeve of her T-shirt for emphasis. She turned to Katie. "You could tell right off we were from Oregon, couldn't you?"

"No," Katie said, swatting the air with her hand. "You

guys all look like naturals around here. You fit in great."

Randy returned just then with a tray heaped with another sandwich, three drinks, a mound of French fries, and a large bowl of swirled frozen yogurt.

"Where did you find the yogurt?" Vicki said, reaching over and taking off the top swirl with her finger. "This is good. You want some, Amy?"

Whether Amy wanted any or not, she followed Vicki to the self-serve machine in the far right corner.

"What about you, Randy?" Katie asked. "Do you want a tour of the dorms, or are you going with the others to the pool?"

"I'd like to see the music building," he said, chomping into his sandwich. After a few quick chews and a swallow, he added, "That is, after I finish eating."

"Of course," Katie agreed. "First things first. And with most of the guys I know around here, food comes first— especially with Doug. Did I tell you he and Tracy come up every Thursday night to lead a Bible study?"

"You're kidding!" Sierra said. "Doug and Tracy. How are they doing?"

"Great. Cutest little married couple you've ever seen. We're calling our group the God-Lovers II, after the original group that started down in San Diego a couple of years ago."

"That must have been the group Tawni went to with Jeremy," Sierra said.

"Oh, that reminds me," Katie said. "I almost forgot. I called Tawni, and she said you guys were planning to stay at her place tonight. But if you want, you can stay here. I found a couple of people who are going home for the weekend, and they volunteered their rooms for you guys. It's up to you.

Tawni said to call her. If you stay here, she'll come up to visit you."

"I'd love to stay," Sierra said. "I'll see what everyone else thinks."

"Do these meal passes work for dinner, too?" Randy asked.

Katie laughed. "No, sorry. But there's a barbecued rib place in town I've heard is good. We could all go there, if you wanted."

Vicki and Amy returned with their frozen yogurt and a guy. Vicki appeared pleased with the yogurt, and Amy didn't look any too disappointed with the guy.

"This is Antonio," Amy said, smiling up at the dark-eyed, good-looking escort. But Mr. Tall, Dark, and Handsome wasn't returning Amy's affectionate gaze. He was staring at Sierra.

"*Bella* Sierra," he said in his rich Italian accent. "It has been so long." With that he leaned over and brushed a kiss across both of Sierra's blushing cheeks.

Sierra caught Amy's surprised expression and felt a need to quickly explain. "How are you doing, Antonio? I haven't seen you since the wedding last summer. Did you meet my friends, Amy and Vicki? And this is Randy," Sierra added.

Randy, his mouth full, nodded amiably at Antonio.

"Antonio rescued us at the yogurt machine," Vicki said, holding up her overflowing cup of yogurt. "Look at this mess! I couldn't get it to stop coming out."

"Katie told me you were coming," Antonio said, sitting down across from Sierra and Randy. He gave Katie a wink. "Have you told them our surprise?"

Sierra immediately suspected something of a romance was brewing between Antonio and Katie. Katie had kept no secret about how she was interested in Antonio last year. They made a cute couple, in that Antonio would bait Katie by pretending his English was insufficient, and she would fall for it every time and correct his mixed-up sentences. The only thing that seemed unusual now was that, if a romantic link existed between them, neither of them acted like it.

"Thanks a lot, Antonio," Katie said. "I was trying to keep the little surprise a surprise but now . . ."

"I didn't say anything," he said, holding up his hands.

"Nice try," Sierra said. "It's no good, though. One of you has to tell us now."

Antonio leaned forward. "You are seriously thinking of coming to school here in the fall, aren't you?"

"Well, I . . . I don't know. Until today I hadn't even considered it," Sierra said.

"I'm interested," Randy said. "If they have a decent music department. The food passes my inspection."

Sierra motioned to Randy that he had a little smear of mayonnaise on the side of his lip. He reached for a napkin and wiped it off. "Is it always this good?" he asked.

Antonio nodded. "We eat well around here."

Katie pinched her side as if measuring her fat. She was so athletic and energetic Sierra couldn't imagine any flab under her baggy white shirt. "They call it the Freshman Fifteen. That's how many pounds you gain your first year here. Even if you enter as a sophomore, like me."

"My cousin said she gained only 10 her first year," Vicki said, licking her spoon and dipping it back into the cup of frozen yogurt.

"She must have gone to a state school," Katie said with a grin. "Here it's definitely a minimum of 15."

Sierra began to feel those tremors of terror again. She had

never tried to lose weight before, since her late-blooming tomboy figure had remained pretty constant until the last six or eight months. It was disturbing to be told she would gain weight when she went to college. That meant another area of her life where she would have to be responsible and disciplined.

"You guys," Sierra said, eager to redirect the conversation, "I believe you're attempting to change the subject. Go back to that surprise Antonio mentioned. What's the big secret?"

Katie and Antonio looked at each other. Antonio raised his eyebrows as if to give Katie the go-ahead.

"It's about Christy and Todd," Katie began.

Before she could go on, Sierra clapped her hand over her mouth to keep from screaming in public.

chapter sixteen

"*N*O, NO, NO!" KATIE SAID QUICKLY. "IT'S NOT what you think. They haven't announced their engagement. At least not yet. At least that I know of. But then, I'm always the last to know everything."

"Who are Todd and Christy?" Vicki asked.

"Don't you remember?" Amy said, the wounded tone still in her voice. "Sierra's friend Christy is the one who took her to Switzerland last summer."

"Actually, Christy's Aunt Marti took us, but, yes, Christy is the one I went to Switzerland with. Todd is her boyfriend. They've been together forever. Only she's at school in Switzerland now, and he's over here. Isn't he about ready to graduate from college?"

Katie shook her head. "Let's just say that Todd's educational path has been a winding one. He's not going to school right now. He's working two different jobs to put some money in the bank."

"He'll start his senior year in the fall," Antonio added. "And where, might you ask, would Todd have chosen to finish his college years but here, at Rancho Corona."

"And," Katie quickly added, flashing her green eyes at

Antonio, "the rest of the surprise news, which somebody couldn't keep to himself, is that Christy has been accepted here, too. This September, we're all going to be back together again."

"Oh, man, you guys are going to have such great times together!" Sierra said, remembering the closeness she felt with this group of friends. Even though all of them were older than she, they had never made her feel younger or left out.

"You guys?" Katie repeated, motioning to Sierra, Randy, Vicki, and Amy. "How about all of us guys. The four of you included. Oh, and Wes, too. You have to come here now. All of you. You have no choice."

"We probably should at least look at a catalog," Vicki said, laughing at Katie's command to them. "I mean, the campus and the student body are great. None of us would argue with you there. But those aren't the areas my parents are going to ask about when I get home."

"Some information packets are waiting for you back at the admin building," Katie said. "I should have given them to you when you first arrived. Sorry about that. We could pick them up now, and then you could check out the pool or Dishner Hall or whatever."

"Let's go," Randy said, getting up and taking his empty tray with him. "Where do I put this?"

"Over here," Antonio said. "Are you the one who wants to see Dishner Hall?"

"If that's the music building, yes."

"I'll show you around," Antonio said.

Making their way out of the cafeteria, Sierra noticed Amy still appeared to have a cloud hanging over her. Was she disappointed that Antonio didn't volunteer to go to the pool with her and Vicki?

Katie led them back to the admin building, where Dawn handed each of them an information packet. They were about to go their separate ways when Wes entered the lobby. He had a calm smile on his face. Sierra knew his meeting with the financial adviser had gone well.

After introducing Antonio to Wes, Sierra asked, "What's next on your schedule? Have you eaten yet?"

"We can recommend the food here," Randy said.

"I thought I'd head over to the cafeteria," Wes said. "I have an appointment with an adviser at 2:30. What do you think? Should we all meet back here?"

Sierra gave Wes the information about their being invited to stay on campus rather than at Tawni's, if they wanted to. Wes asked the others, and everyone was eager to stay except Amy. She said it was fine, but then she added quietly, "So, we're probably not going to the beach, then." She wasn't making a big deal about it, though obviously she had been hoping. And Sierra couldn't blame her. If she had never been to the beach in Southern California, Sierra knew she would be sad about the missed opportunity, too.

They quickly made their plans. Wes would call Tawni, all of them would meet back at the van at 5:30, and Wes would drive them to this barbecued rib place Katie recommended. They would stay in the dorms that night, and the next day, Saturday, they would head home and try to visit at least one more university campus on the way. Wes was adamant that he had to be back in Corvallis by 7:00 Monday morning because he couldn't miss his first class. Knowing how long the drive home would be made all of them understand Wesley's concern about staying around too long on Saturday.

The group split up, and Katie directed Sierra toward the dorm.

As soon as they were out of hearing distance from the others, Sierra said, "Katie, whatever happened between you and Antonio? I thought you two were getting pretty interested in each other."

"Tonio and me?" A glimmer of remembrance came over Katie's face. "Oh, yeah. Last year. That's ancient history."

"What happened?"

"Nothing," Katie said with a laugh. "That's exactly what happened. Nothing! Antonio is a big flirt, in case you hadn't noticed. Somehow I was the last girl on the planet to realize that all the sweet talk and kisses on the cheek were his way of communicating with everyone. Well, at least with all the girls." She shook her head. "I've always been a slow learner when it comes to guys. I really believed he thought I was something special. Then one day I finally woke up, hit my head on the headboard, and the dream was over."

"That's too bad," Sierra said sympathetically. "I think the two of you made a darling couple."

"So did everyone else," Katie said. "Try not getting your hopes up about a guy when everyone is telling you that. Here we are."

Katie gestured toward a long, three-story dormitory. It was built in the same early California style as the rest of the campus. She slipped a plastic card through the security lock at the front, and the wide double doors opened automatically.

The first sight that caught Sierra's attention was the court area in the middle of the rectangular building. It appeared more like the lobby of an exotic hotel than a women's dormitory. The patio was paved with red tiles and filled with a garden of tall trees, under which sat benches around a small fountain.

"How beautiful," Sierra murmured. "This is where you live?"

"Yep. This is Sophia Hall, named after Mr. Perez's wife."

"And who is Mr. Perez?" Sierra asked, following Katie past several students, who all greeted Katie.

"Didn't I tell you that part on the tour? Oh, no! They're going to fire me as campus guide. I forgot to tell you the history of this place." Katie stopped in the middle of the courtyard, next to the fountain, and took a deep breath. "Sometime in the 1920s or '30s—I'm not real good with dates—all this property was owned by a man named Miguel Perez. He and his wife tried to start an orange grove here on top of the mesa. It didn't work out because there was a drought or something. He gave up on trees and started to raise cattle instead."

"How did he get the cows up here?" Sierra asked.

Katie gave her a funny look. "I don't know. They had trucks back then, you know. Anyway, Mr. Perez promised the Lord that he would give half the profit from his cattle ranch back to God, and he did. For years the ranch did a fantastic business and half the profits went to Christian organizations. One of them was the Open Bible College of Los Angeles."

"I've heard of that college," Sierra said.

"I guess it was *the* Christian college of its day. Rancho Corona is actually a satellite of OBCLA because, when Mr. Perez died, he didn't have any living children, so he left everything to OBCLA."

"What a nice gift!" Sierra said. "I take it his ranch was called Rancho Corona?"

"Actually, the Perez ranch was originally called El Rancho de la Cruz y la Corona."

"The ranch of the what?" Sierra said, attempting to translate the Spanish words.

"The Ranch of the Cross and the Crown. A stained-glass window in the chapel has the ranch symbol on it. It's a cross with a gold crown resting on it. It's really pretty. I'll have to show you the chapel before you leave."

"And which room is yours?" Sierra asked, looking up at the long row of dorm rooms that lined the three floors.

"Second floor. Follow me."

Katie's room wasn't very large. There was a shared desk in the center of the room with a bookcase to the ceiling that separated the two sides. The twin beds were against opposite walls, and the closets were built in on either side of the door. Sierra was surprised at how barracklike it seemed. The suite-style rooms at Valencia Hills were much nicer.

It was easy to guess which side of the room was Katie's. Her decorations were minimal, and her bulletin board was covered with photos, many of them of people Sierra had met. She stepped closer to the wall to examine the collage and was surprised to see one of herself there. It was in front of the big wooden front doors at Carnforth Hall, where they had met in England. Next to Sierra's face was one of the large lion's head door knockers.

"I remember when you took that," Sierra said. "I still have that jacket."

"And do you still have those cowboy boots?" Katie asked, pointing to another group picture in which Sierra's legs were dangling over the edge of a stone wall, and her cowboy boots were very noticeable.

"Yep. I still have them, and I still wear them." Sierra pointed to another picture. "When was this one taken? That's you and Christy, isn't it? You look so young."

Katie leaned closer to examine the picture of the two of them wearing big T-shirts. Both of them had their hair up on top of their heads, and they were holding a large bag of M&M's. She laughed. "That was at a sleepover when we were 15." She looked closer. "That wasn't the party where we first became friends, I don't think. It was probably the next one we went to together."

"It's so neat that you and Christy go way back."

"What about you and Vicki and Amy?"

"We get along great now, but we didn't used to be friends at all. At least not all three of us at the same time. We've only been doing things together for a few months. That's why I think it's great you and Christy have been friends for so long."

"And it's only going to get better in the fall when she comes to school here. We've already signed up to be roommates. We'll have such a great time with you and all your friends," Katie said.

Sierra plopped down on Katie's bed. "You make it sound so easy."

"Why not?" Katie said. "I mean, why wouldn't you want to come to school here?"

"I don't know. It's so expensive."

"So? You pray about it; apply for every grant, scholarship, and loan they'll let you apply for; and then get into a work-study program, like me, and earn your spending money while you're at school."

"What's your work-study program?" Sierra asked.

"I'm an agronomy major, if you can believe it. I know it's weird. Ever since I first studied plants in high school science, I've been strangely attracted to finding out how things work within nature. They have me in a work-study course where I work in the organic garden 10 hours a week. I didn't show it to you. It's terraced down the side of the hill by the pool. We sell a lot of our organic vegetables at the Saturday farmer's market in town."

"That sounds like a lot of fun."

"I like it. For my next project I want to develop my own brand of herbal tea. I should have shown you the garden. I already have all my herbs planted, and some of them are coming up nicely." Katie dropped into her beanbag chair and said, "What's your major going to be?"

"Communications, I think. I had to put something on the forms, and that's what I'm most interested in right now."

"Perfect!" Katie said. "Rancho has the best communications department around. Radio, video, journalism, anything you're interested in. And last year their debate team placed second in the national tournament. I can see you as Rancho's star debater, bringing home all the trophies."

Sierra gave her exuberant friend a skeptical smile.

Katie cocked her head and eyed Sierra suspiciously. "It's not about money or majors, is it?"

Sierra shrugged.

"Okay. I get it. What's his name, and where's he going to school?"

Sierra was surprised at Katie's perceptiveness. Letting down her guard, Sierra smiled softly. "Paul's at the University of Edinburgh now. I don't know where he'll be in the fall."

Katie looked confused for only a moment. Then, with the dawn of recognition across her face, she said, "Paul, huh? Isn't he the one who saw you walking in the rain that one time with your arms full of flowers?"

Sierra nodded. "Daffodils. He still calls me the Daffodil Queen sometimes."

"Still, huh. Are you two together?"

Sierra shook her head. "We write each other once or twice a month. That's all. You know he's Jeremy's brother, don't you?"

"Tawni's boyfriend?" Katie asked, leaning forward. "Ah, the plot thickens. This could be interesting."

"Except there's nothing to tell. I'm not even sure why I mentioned him. He said he was coming back to the States at the end of June. I was just, I don't know . . ."

"Dreaming a little dream?" Katie concluded for her. "Wishing a little wish? Praying a little prayer that you would end up at the same college?"

"Something like that," Sierra said, trying hard to catch her imagination before it took off like a kite.

"It could happen," Katie said with a grin. "I mean, look at Todd and Christy. God can move mountains when He wants to."

"I know," Sierra agreed. Katie's mentioning mountains got Sierra thinking about when they had driven past Mount Shasta and how it was cloaked in thick fog. "And then again, God can also hide mountains when He wants to."

chapter seventeen

"Y OU'LL HAVE TO DIRECT ME, KATIE, ONCE WE GET down the hill," Wes called out in the noisy van of people.

"Turn right at the first light you come to, go about a mile, and it's on the right side. Sam's Barbecue Pit."

Katie was in the middle seat with Amy and Antonio. Vicki was in the front; and Randy, Sierra, and Tawni were in the snore zone. Tawni had driven up to spend the evening with them and had appeared especially glad to see Sierra.

"What do you think of Rancho?" Tawni asked. She had moved to Southern California to begin a modeling career last summer. It hadn't turned out to be as glamorous or wonderful as Tawni had imagined, but she was doing well and seemed to still be glad to be out on her own.

"It's great," Sierra said. "What do you think? Should I come here?"

"That's up to you," Tawni said.

"You gave up on going to school in Reno, didn't you?" Sierra asked.

Tawni nodded. Her hair was pulled up in a French twist, and when she nodded, some of the strands on the sides fell down. Her hair color had been different every time Sierra had seen her lately. This time it was a caramel blonde, similar to Sierra's hair. The sisterly resemblance stopped there, though, since Tawni was adopted.

"I can't believe I hatched that scheme to go to school in Reno just so I could meet Lina," Tawni said. Tawni had found her birth mother and discovered she was a professor at the University of Nevada, Reno. Tawni had written her a letter, but when Tawni didn't hear back right away, she made plans to enroll at UNR. However, Lina Rasmussen did write back, though not right away. She initiated a meeting for the two of them last fall, and since then she and Tawni had seen each other twice and called each other every week or so.

"Did Jeremy tell you that Paul is planning to come back to the States at the end of June?" Sierra said.

"No. When did Paul tell you?"

"I got a letter last week."

"I still don't understand why you and Paul write letters instead of send e-mails to each other. Paul sends e-mails to Jeremy all the time."

Sierra smiled quietly to herself. Written letters were so much more romantic and thoughtful. It took time to take pen in hand and compose a newsy yet tender letter. And right now, that gift of time and effort was all Sierra had to give Paul. She knew that was exactly the same kind of sacrifice he was making when he wrote to her.

"What is Paul going to do when he comes back?" Tawni asked.

"He didn't say. I don't think he knows yet."

"Hmm."

"What?" Sierra asked.

"Nothing. I'm curious about what Paul's going to do. Jeremy says most of his friends are transferring here next fall."

"Tell me about it," Sierra quipped.

"Where are we going for dinner?" Tawni asked.

Before Sierra could answer, Wes pulled the van into the crowded parking lot toward which Katie directed him. The sign over the restaurant said, "Sam's BBQ Pit—Best Ribs This Side of Texas."

"This is it?" Tawni said. "Seriously?"

"Must be the place," Sierra said as the rest of the gang began to roll out of the van.

"When Wes called and said we were going out to dinner, this isn't exactly what I had in mind." Tawni extracted her long legs from the back of the van, and Sierra followed her.

"This place is hoppin'!" Katie exclaimed when the group entered the small restaurant.

She had to yell over the country music blaring from the speakers in the ceiling. Long picnic tables lined the right side of the restaurant, and the counter where customers stood to place their orders took up the left side.

"Surely there's another place to eat in this town," Tawni said.

"I've heard good things about this place," Katie hollered back. Undaunted, she led the way to the counter and began to order.

"I guess we're stuck," Tawni said. "Do you see any salads on the menu?"

The menu consisted of one thing: ribs. The only selection customers had was exactly how many ribs they wanted. There was the Cowpoke Plate for kids that came with six ribs, the Rustler Plate that came with 12 ribs, the Hired Hand Plate with 18 ribs, and the Rancher Special that came with 24 ribs and free seconds.

Tawni and Amy skeptically ordered the Cowpoke Plate,

but the server objected, saying they weren't under 12 years old. Katie stepped in and, with her quick tongue and friendly smile, convinced the employee to let them go for the kid's plate. According to Katie, it would be the kid's plate or nothing for these two, and if Sam wanted their business, he had better let up on the age rule.

Sierra ordered the Rustler. She paid for it and then moved through the cafeteria-style line to pick up her tray behind Vicki, who had ordered the same thing. Both of them were shocked when they saw the amount of food on the trays. The ribs alone took up the whole plate. On a side plate came the "fixin's," which included baked beans, cold slaw, corn on the cob, and a thick hunk of white bread.

"I feel like Fred Flintstone!" Sierra exclaimed as she followed Vicki to the picnic table where the others were already seated. "If we were at a drive-in restaurant with one of those window trays, the car would tip over."

"I think I'm going to tip over," Vicki said. "There's no way I can eat all this."

"Aren't we glad we brought Randy, the human disposal," Sierra said.

"Great choice of restaurant," Wes said to Katie when they were all seated. He and Randy had ordered the Rancher Special, and each of them had to carry two trays to hold it all. Wes offered to pray for the food. Their table was the farthest from the speakers, which was good because the music wasn't quite so loud at their end of the restaurant. They could actually hear each other speak.

"Don't you think it would be more appropriate if we prayed for forgiveness for being a bunch of gluttons?" Katie asked.

Wes laughed and suggested they hold hands while they

prayed. Sierra noticed that Wes was sitting next to Katie.

With a round of "Amens," the group took to the ribs like ravenous beasts. All but Tawni and Amy. They both tried to use plastic knives and forks to cut the heavily sauced meat from the bone.

"Oh, come on," Katie teased. "You're not supposed to whittle those bones into figurines. Get aggressive! Stuff them in your face." To demonstrate she picked up a rib with both hands and took a big chomp out if it. The barbecue sauce dripped down her chin and onto her tray.

"You have a little something right there," Wes said, pointing to Katie's chin after her demonstration.

With her hands covered with barbecue sauce, Katie said, "Oh, really?" She reached over and made a red smear across Wes's cheek. "You have a little something on your face, too."

To Sierra's surprise, Wes cracked up. He returned the favor and painted a streak on each of Katie's cheeks. She then evened out his war paint by marking his other cheek. Vicki and Antonio laughed the hardest at Wes's and Katie's antics. Sierra laughed and joked with the others, but she felt that strange sensation in her stomach that she got when she thought Amy liked Wes. Now it was Katie instead of Amy who was getting Wes's attention.

Drawing inward, Sierra nibbled on her corn on the cob and gave herself a lecture about giving in to these immature jealousy fits over her brother. She needed to stop feeling so possessive. Sierra knew she couldn't spend the rest of her life examining the motives of every girl who appeared interested in Wes.

Picking up her glass of milk and taking a long drink, Sierra resolved to put away her childish insecurities about Wesley. She decided if she considered him more of a buddy than her adored brother during this stage of their lives, she would be less likely to feel she was selecting whom he could date. The funny thing was, Wes wasn't dating anyone and hadn't been for a long time, as far as Sierra knew. Maybe she was afraid that since he was getting older, his dating choices would be more like potential marriage choices, and she wanted somehow to be involved in that selection.

Now she realized it wasn't her choice. It wasn't her life; it was Wesley's. Her role was to love and support him. And the only way she could do that was to let go of all these assumptions and expectations.

Strangely, the mental exercise increased Sierra's appetite, and she went after her ribs with renewed gusto.

"Do you suppose they actually serve ribs like these in Texas?" Antonio asked. He was seated across from Sierra and seemed to be directing his question to Amy, who was sitting next to him on the long bench.

"I don't know. I've never been there."

"Neither have I," Antonio said, reaching for a napkin from the stack in the middle of the table. "Where I come from in Italy, you would never see such ribs."

"What part of Italy are you from?" Amy asked.

"The north. Near Lake Como. Have you heard of it?"

"My uncle is from that area. I don't remember the name of the town. He runs an Italian restaurant in Portland." Amy gave Antonio one of her best smiles and said, "I think you would like his restaurant. The food is very good."

As Sierra watched, Amy and Antonio launched into a lively conversation about Italian food. Turning her attention to Tawni, Sierra said, "What do you think?"

"What do I think about what?" Tawni asked. She had

broken off a corner of her white bread and was eating it without butter.

"What do you think about this Texas food? Do you like it?"

"It's okay. I'd probably enjoy it more if I didn't know how loaded it was with fats and carbos. I have a magazine shoot next week. That means rabbit food the rest of the weekend for me."

"Don't you hate that? Having to worry about your weight and how you look every minute of every day?"

"I try not to worry about it," Tawni said. "I don't think I do as much as I used to. It's part of the career I've chosen. If I were an athlete, I'd have to work out every day to be good at my sport. As a model, I have to spend time on my appearance. But that's not all I do every minute of every day."

"I didn't mean to imply it was," Sierra said, thinking of all the warnings about gaining weight as a college freshman. "I was just thinking it would be a pain to have to watch what you ate all the time."

"It is sometimes," Tawni said, sounding less defensive. "I guess anything in life can be a pain. We all end up choosing the level of pain we can endure to reach our goals."

"You're right," Sierra said. "That's profound." She wasn't used to having Tawni share such thoughts with her.

"You know who told me that?" Tawni said, wiping her fingers daintily and pushing away her plate.

"Jeremy?"

Tawni shook her head. "No, it was Lina. Lina told me that was why she gave me up for adoption. You know she was only 15 when she got pregnant with me, and her boyfriend was no longer in the picture by the time she found out. Lina said she wanted what was best for me and didn't think at that point in her life she could offer me the same things adoptive parents could. She said her goal was to finish school and become a college professor, which she did."

"I imagine giving you up for adoption was the deepest level of pain for her," Sierra said. "But I'm glad she did. Otherwise you and I never would have been sisters."

A tear formed in the corner of Tawni's eye and threatened to tumble down her perfectly made-up face. "That is so sweet of you to say, Sierra." Tawni reached over and gave Sierra a hug. "I don't know if I've ever said this really clearly to you, but I'm glad we're sisters—very glad."

"I am, too." Sierra's words were whispered into her sister's ear as the two of them hugged and cried just a little.

In the background, honky-tonk music blared, and Sam's rib slabs sizzled on the grill. It was an unlikely setting for such a bonding moment. But Sierra knew it was a moment she would never forget.

chapter eighteen

SIERRA AWOKE EARLY THE NEXT MORNING WITH A STOM-
achache. She wasn't sure if it was from the ribs she
ate at Sam's or if it was from all the junk food she
had scarfed afterward when they all went back to the Student
Center and hung out in the lounge, talking until almost
midnight.

Getting up quietly, Sierra peeked over at Katie, who was
still sound asleep. Dawn, Katie's roommate, had offered to
let Sierra sleep in her bed, but it had been too soft for Sierra,
making it a night of restlessness. So many thoughts, feelings,
and ideas were bouncing off the walls of Sierra's mind that
she decided to dress and go for a walk. She knew it would be
useless to try to sleep anymore. She would much rather greet
the day by trying to glimpse the elusive blue Pacific from the
deck of the Student Center.

Slipping into her jeans and a sweatshirt, Sierra pulled her
hair back in a clip and quietly left Katie's dorm room. No
one else appeared to be awake yet. The halls and lobby were
empty. And why should any reasonable college student be
up? The sun had barely risen this Saturday morning. Sierra
quietly opened the double doors and exited into the new day.

Once outside she immediately felt better. Perhaps her

feelings soared because of the brisk morning air or the sweet fragrance of honeysuckle that wafted in her direction from the vine covering the far side of the building. Maybe it was the night sky just beginning to fade into a rosy shade of aqua that lifted her up. Whatever it was, Sierra drew the refreshing sensation into her lungs and headed toward the Student Center with light, energetic steps. A car engine revved in the student parking lot and passed her on the road a few minutes later. The driver, a young woman, gave a little beep and waved at Sierra as if she knew her.

That was one of the many things Sierra liked about Rancho Corona. The students were friendly and open. She rounded the back of the Student Center and took the steps up to the deck two at a time. Her efforts were well rewarded. Morning had come to the top of the mesa only minutes before Sierra arrived on the deck. The faithful sun now rose steadily behind her. Before her lay the campus, spread out like a picnic on green fields all the way to the end of the mesa. After that, far in the distance, laced with morning clouds as thin as a whisper, lay the vast, blue Pacific Ocean. The immensity of the view and the vividness of the early morning colors stunned Sierra. She felt a shiver, partly from the chill of the breeze and partly from the astounding beauty of it all.

At the edge of the campus, away from the other buildings and near a grove of trees, Sierra noticed a small, white building with a spired roof. She guessed it was the chapel Katie had mentioned. Tracing the horizon with her hungry eyes, Sierra ate up the scenery. It was almost too beautiful to take in—a glorious glut of wonder.

Filled but not satisfied, Sierra left the deck and scampered through the wet grass toward the chapel. She felt like laughing aloud because her spirit was so light. Pausing along the trail only for a moment, Sierra snatched up a dandelion. She closed her eyes, made a wish, and then blew all the feathery hairs from the dandelion's head and watched them dance away on the morning breeze.

Sierra knew if anyone could see her at this moment, wishing on dandelions and fairly skipping down the path, they would label her as loony and anything but college-student material. But it was unlikely anyone on this campus was up yet, and if he were, he probably had something more important to do than watch a young heart celebrate the new day.

That's how Sierra felt: forever young in her heart. All the thoughts and feelings she had wrestled with in her sleep that had weighed so heavily upon her felt light at this moment. So many things had felt so intense these past few days, and her spirit had been unsettled. But not now, not on this morning with its promise of so much life to be lived.

Skipping along, Sierra came to where the path ended, at the door of the solemn, silent chapel. She tried the door and found it unlocked. Entering with reverence, she shuffled to the front and sat down on one of the cushioned, wooden benches. At the front of the chapel was a beautifully carved altar with a large, open Bible on the top of it. Behind the altar was a stained-glass window that shone brighter and brighter as each ray of morning light poured through it, sending its pattern and colors into a dim reflection on the floor at Sierra's feet.

She stared a long time at the stained-glass window. It was just as Katie had described it. A thick, brown cross slanted to the right, and around the horizontal portion of the cross hung a golden crown studded with bright jewels.

"Father," Sierra whispered into the sacred air around her,

"thank You. Thank You for sending Your Son to die for me. Thank You for making a way for me to come to You through Him. Thank You for forgiving all my sins when I surrendered my life to Christ. Thank You for giving me eternal life. I know if I can trust You with all that, I should be able to trust You with all these anxious thoughts and feelings that kept me from sleeping last night."

Sierra glanced around the small chapel before continuing. God felt so close to her here, at this moment. She almost expected to see His shadow on the wall. "I guess I'm worried about the future. I don't think I ever have been worried about it before—at least not like this. Part of me wants to go away to college, particularly a college like this. Another part of me doesn't want to leave home. I don't want to have to be so responsible. I know I've had it easy. I guess I like my life at home more than I realized. I don't think I'm ready to grow up."

Sierra rubbed her hands together. It was chilly in the little chapel. "I feel as though I didn't finish a lot of things in life when I could have. Like with Tawni. Last night, when she hugged me, I felt bad that I'd wasted all those years when she was at home. Why weren't we close friends then? And then there's Amy. Did You hear her last night? Of course You did. It really bugged me when Antonio asked her when she became a Christian and she said she wasn't necessarily one of us. Why isn't her heart open to You, God? What happened?"

For another five minutes Sierra poured her heart out to the Lord. She had unsettled feelings about Warner, fears about maintaining her high GPA through this last semester, questions about how she was supposed to know which school God wanted her to go to, or if it was His plan for her to stay home. She knew all too well that she was an impetuous person. This was one time in her life when her decisions mattered a lot. She couldn't make a snap choice. Her future was at stake.

When all her doubts, fears, and worries were poured out, she stopped talking and waited, listening to the silence. The emotional exercise left her exhausted, and she stretched out on the pew. Within minutes she was asleep.

The sound of the chapel door opening and quick footsteps woke her sometime later. Sierra sat bolt upright and startled the man who had entered. He let out a funny gasping sound and then apologized for disturbing Sierra.

"No, it's okay. I was just leaving. Do you know what time it is?" Sierra squinted in the brightened chapel and stretched her kinked neck.

"Nine-thirty," the man said. He looked like one of the professors and carried a Bible and notebook under one arm.

"Thank you." Sierra straightened her sweatshirt and hurried past the man. She jogged across the campus, not sure where to go first. If the others were up, which she was sure they were, they were probably out looking for her. The best tactic, she figured, was to go back to Katie's room.

When she reached the front door of Sophia Hall, Sierra had to wait for someone with a security card to come along and open the door. She sprinted down the second-floor hall and knocked once on Katie's door before opening it. Katie wasn't there.

Sierra was about to leave when she noticed a note on the bed. It read, *Sierra, where are you, girl? If you come back here, call 240 on the phone at the end of the hall. That's Security. Tell them you're here and for them to page us. Katie.*

Hurrying to the phone, Sierra followed Katie's instructions. The person who answered and took the information said, "Where were you? Katie had us looking all over campus for the last hour."

"I'm sorry. I was in the chapel."

"Oh," was all the person on the other end said. "I'll page Katie and tell her you're waiting for her in her room."

Sierra went back to the room and quickly packed her things. She hoped her brother wouldn't be too upset with her for putting everyone in a panic. Wes had wanted to leave early this morning. Nine-thirty wasn't exactly early in his book.

Katie's dorm-room door opened with a blast of people all firing questions at Sierra at once. She tried her best to explain that she had been praying and fell asleep.

Vicki seemed to be the most understanding. "We're glad you're okay," she said. "Wes said he would pull the van around in front of the dorm so we can get going. Do you have all your stuff?"

"It's right here. Is he upset?"

Vicki shrugged. "I think he's okay. He was worried. We all were. You just disappeared."

"I didn't mean to fall asleep," Sierra explained to Wes a few minutes later as she loaded her gear into the van. "I'm sorry."

"It's okay," he said. "Next time leave a note."

"Or at least a lock of hair and a trail of bread crumbs," Katie said, still appearing flustered over the whole event. "It doesn't look good on my record as a campus host when I lose visitors. We had half the campus out looking for you. I wouldn't be surprised if your name appears in a tabloid somewhere tomorrow under the headline, 'Campus Visitor Abducted by Aliens.'"

Katie's humor helped to clear the tension with Wes and

the others. Then another tension surfaced. It was time to say good-bye. Katie kept making jokes, trying to make light of the situation. They all hugged her, and Antonio gave the women his trademark kiss across their cheeks.

"So, e-mail me sometime and tell me what you decide, okay, Sierra?" Katie said. "Or just e-mail Christy. She'll make sure I get the message."

"I'll e-mail you," Sierra said. "And I'll give Christy a hard time for not telling me she was planning to come here." Sierra climbed into the van behind Vicki. "Bye, and thanks for everything."

Sierra stared at every tree and every building as they drove off campus. It was quiet in the van, and she wondered if the others were trying to memorize every detail of the campus as she was. Or were they upset at her for wandering off and producing a Goldilocks-nap story to explain her actions. Once they had driven under the entrance sign and passed the stone pillars, Sierra apologized to everyone again.

"Don't worry about it," Wes said, catching her eye in the rearview mirror. "It's no big deal. We need to make some plans from here on out, though. The rest of us talked at breakfast, and now we need your input. Do you still want to visit another campus?"

"I guess. I don't know. Do we need to just drive straight home? What does everyone else want to do?"

"Hit the beach," Vicki said with a grin. "Wes says he's checked the map, and we can visit one of the colleges on the way to the beach and then head home. What do you think?"

"I'm all for going to the beach," Sierra said.

"That's what we thought you would say," Randy said. He turned around in the front seat, and with a more serious expression, he said, "Are you going to apply to Rancho?"

Sierra felt caught off guard. "I don't know. Are you?"

Randy nodded. "Yes, I think I am. I hadn't thought much about going away to college. I thought I'd stick around Portland. But Rancho has an amazing music program. Did you know they even have a recording studio on campus? It's the best setup I've seen yet."

"What about you, Wes? How did all your meetings go?" Sierra asked.

"Great. I'm pretty sure this is where I'll end up. I never imagined you would want to come here, Sierra."

Sierra tried to evaluate Wes's tone. Would he find it annoying to have his kid sister running around campus as a freshman when he was there for graduate school? She turned to Amy and Vicki and asked what they thought about going to Rancho.

"It's a pretty big decision," Vicki said. "I liked everything I saw. My parents will go over the catalog, and I know they'll want to know what Rancho has that no other school in Oregon can offer. I'm sure I'll have to come up with a scholarship or a grant or something."

"I'd have to get a scholarship, too," Sierra said. She dreaded the thought of presenting her parents with more paperwork after they had already filled out endless forms for her. But she hadn't even known Rancho existed then.

Amy was sitting quietly in the back. Sierra reached over the seat and gave Amy's leg a friendly squeeze. "What are you thinking? Would you want to apply to Rancho Corona?"

"I don't think so," she said in a low voice.

"Why not? What didn't you like about it?"

"Nothing. It's a great school. I just don't think it's for me."

"Why not? If we all end up applying, you might as well apply, too."

"Sierra, give it up," Amy snapped. "I'm not interested, okay? Can't you leave it at that?"

"Okay," Sierra said, still looking Amy in the eye. Sierra waited a full minute before saying, "Don't you think you can at least tell me why?"

"No."

That was the last word they heard out of Amy all the way to the next campus they were to scout out.

chapter nineteen

*T*HE COLLEGE CAMPUS TOUR TURNED OUT TO BE A QUICK one. It was a small college nestled in the middle of an L.A. suburb. Wes drove through the campus, and Randy ran out and picked up a catalog from the admissions office. Few students were around, since it was noon on Saturday and the weather was exceptionally nice and warm. Vicki said she guessed everyone had gone to the beach, and she was glad they were headed there, too.

Sierra had been to Newport Beach several times, but she hadn't been to Huntington, which was the beach Wes drove to. He said he had been there before with his friend Ryan and that it was nice, long, and wide. As they climbed out of the van, they realized it was much warmer inland than it was on the coast. A thin layer of fog hung over the horizon, and a strong breeze whipped Sierra's long curls into her face.

"Why is it so cold?" Amy said. "I was all set to put on my bathing suit, but this is as cold as the beaches in Oregon."

"It's spring, you know. It's not summer yet," Wes said. "Look, those surfers even have on wet suits."

"It's pretty here," Vicki said cheerfully. She reached for her sweatshirt before Wes closed and locked the doors.

"Wait. I want my sweatshirt, too," Sierra said.

"Me, too," Amy said. "And I want a pair of socks."

"Socks?" Randy said. "You don't wear socks to the beach. You have to go barefoot. Once your feet get in the sand, they'll warm up."

"Oh, like you would know," Vicki said, punching Randy in the arm. "You're such a beach bum."

"Hey, I saw it in a movie. They ran along the beach in the winter and buried their feet in the sand. They were smiling and didn't look cold at all."

"In the movies?" Vicki questioned. "Haven't you ever been to the beach in California before either?"

"Nope," Randy said, stuffing his hands into his pockets. "And I'm beginning to agree with Amy. We could have gone to the coast back in Oregon and been warmer."

"Come on," Sierra said. "We have to at least walk in the sand and put our toes in the water. I can't believe how hot it was inland and how cold it is when you hit the coast."

They huddled close and marched stiffly through the cold sand.

"My feet aren't any warmer," Amy said. "Tell me, Randy, when are my feet supposed to warm up?"

"Maybe we should run," Wes said. He took off jogging before the others had a chance to consider his idea.

Sierra broke from the others and ran after her brother. Several other joggers passed them along the wet sand where Sierra and Wes jogged in unison. A few surfers sat on their boards, waiting for the ocean to churn up a decent wave. Aside from that, very few people were at the beach today. No one sat under an umbrella eating lunch or lazed around soaking up the rays and listening to the radio. It did seem a world away from Newport Beach in the summer, which was how Sierra remembered it.

Sierra and Wes jogged without speaking. Sierra paced her rhythmic breath by Wes's. Their mom was an avid jogger, and all the Jensen kids at one time or another had learned some of her secrets. Sierra knew they had already broken their mom's cardinal rule by not warming up ahead of time.

Wes stopped and motioned to Sierra to turn around and head back. The other three were huddled close together, still walking through the sand toward Wes and Sierra. When they saw Sierra and Wes turn around, they turned, too, and headed back to the van. Sierra was beginning to enjoy the sensation of the cold, firm sand on her bare feet. The wind was to their backs now, and the gusts felt much nicer pushing them forward than when they were in their faces. Even in its chilly, overcast state, the beach exuded a sense of power. The waves roared their way to the shore the same as they did on sunny days. The seagulls still screeched and swooped, even though the trash cans held no snacks for them today. Sierra liked the constancy of the ocean in the midst of one of its many moods. It was still the beach, and it would still be the beach the next time she came to visit it.

"Sure you don't want to go for a swim now?" Wes asked, panting deeply when they all arrived back at the van.

"I'm positive!" Amy said. "Open the door, will you?"

She wore shorts, and her slender legs were covered with goose bumps. The rest of them had on jeans, which might explain why they weren't quite so miserable. But now the bottom edge of Sierra's jeans was wet and sandy. She quickly learned that could be worse than having goose bumps. At least the goose bumps could be rubbed away once everyone jumped into the car and turned on the heater. The wet, sandy jeans would take longer to dry and feel sticky for a long time.

"I liked that," Sierra said after they had driven a few miles down the road. "I'm glad we went."

"It's nothing like in the movies," Randy said.

"Is anyone else hungry?" Wes asked.

"I am," Sierra said. "I seem to have missed breakfast this morning."

Wes stopped at the first fast-food place they came to, which happened to be a Taco Bell. They ordered enough food to host a nice little Mexican fiesta in the van as they kept pushing north. Once again, Randy ate more than the rest of them. He also did the same thing he always did when he and Sierra ate at Lotsa Tacos in Portland. He teased her mercilessly about drinking milk with her tacos.

"It's perfectly normal and very delicious," Sierra said.

"Very delicious," Randy repeated in a high voice. "You sound as though you're in a milk commercial."

"I'd rather be in a milk commercial than in one of your beach movies where people sit around acting warm in the middle of winter."

"Is that rain on the windshield?" Vicki suddenly asked.

Wes started the windshield wipers. "Guess you can tell we're heading home. The Oregon rain missed us so much it's come all the way down here to keep us company."

"That also explains why the beach was so cold," Amy said.

A dull sense of sadness came over them. Their adventure was coming to an end. All that was left were miles and miles of freeway and numerous stops at nondescript gas-station rest rooms.

Vicki found a radio station she liked. Amy went to sleep in the backseat, covering herself with every spare sweatshirt and jacket she could find. Randy sat next to Sierra, looking through the information packet from the various colleges.

Suddenly, he let out a low whistle. "Did you see what

tuition costs for a year at this one?"

Sierra looked over his shoulder at the papers. "That's about the same as what it is at Valencia Hills. Rancho is more."

"More? You're kidding!" Randy looked shocked. "Are you sure there's a way to round up enough scholarship money in time?"

"I don't know. We probably should have started this whole process a lot sooner."

"It's kind of weird," he said, "thinking about going to college. I figured I'd go to Portland State or maybe a community college the first few years."

"That's what Katie did. She and Christy both went to community college their first year. That way they could live at home and save up some money."

Randy shifted in the seat. "Sierra, do you feel old enough to leave home and start being totally responsible for yourself?"

"No," Sierra said, looking closely at Randy. "I thought I was the only one who was feeling that way."

"You? You've already had a few chances to try your wings," Randy said. "Like when you went to Europe and everything. I guess I'm more of a baby than I realized. I didn't think this decision would be here yet."

"Exactly," Sierra said, looking out the rain-streaked window at the other cars zooming past them on the freeway. "I've felt more insecure on this trip than I ever did when I went to Europe. Isn't that strange?"

"Not really. With your other trips, you knew what to expect when you got home. Your parents would be there, and all your needs would be provided for. The thing that gets me about college is the whole money thing. I mean, even if our tuition is covered, what about spending money? Antonio was telling me he works a bunch of odd jobs just to earn some cash so he can do things like eat out with us at Sam's."

"I know," Sierra agreed. "I'm more spoiled than I realized."

"You and me both. If there's anything I learned on this trip, it's that I need to tell my parents how much I appreciate them and all they do for me." Randy stuffed the papers back into the folder. "I mean, I buy my own guitar strings and keep gas in my truck. I thought that was a big responsibility. I don't know what I'm going to do when I have to start paying for my in-between-cafeteria-meals food."

Sierra smiled. "You'll need a full-time job or at least a part-time one that pays well."

"No kidding!"

"Katie said we should look into the work-study programs."

"More paperwork," Randy muttered.

They rolled along in silence. Vicki hummed along with a familiar song on the radio. Sierra fought the urge to panic over the huge decisions that lay before her.

"You know what, Randy?" Sierra lowered her voice and confided in her buddy. "I don't think I'm done being a teenager yet. I don't cherish the idea of becoming an adult. What was that song you were working on? About only having enough light from the headlights to see a little ways down the road?"

"Oh yeah. Our Mount Shasta song. I'm still working on that one."

"Well, I feel as if I'm charging down this road to adulthood, but both my headlights are on dim. It's very hard to see the road."

"Sounds as though your battery is low," Randy said. "It'll be different once you get recharged."

Sierra wondered if Randy meant she needed to get recharged physically or spiritually. Or maybe he meant emotionally. A great deal had happened in the past few days. She stared out the rain-streaked window, feeling the same unsettledness she had experienced earlier that morning when she'd prayed in the chapel. She had expected answers to all her questions to come pouring over her like light through the stained-glass window. Instead, she had fallen asleep. Maybe her battery did need recharging.

Sleep wouldn't come to her right away as they drove home through the rain. Her imagination saw to that. Far too many decisions had to be made. Should she apply to Rancho Corona? What would Wes think if she went there? Was she interested in going there only because all her friends would be there? Was that such a bad reason? What about the finances? Could she get a scholarship? And would she need a part-time job once she started school?

Sierra looked over the seat at Amy stretched out under her pile of sweatshirts, sleeping peacefully. Sierra knew she wouldn't feel settled until she at least knew why her friend had such an adverse reaction to applying at Rancho.

Finally, her imagination floated to Paul. What about that big unknown area in her life? Talk about a road traveled with very little light to show what lies ahead!

"Play me a song," Sierra said to Randy. "Like that first night when I was driving. You have no idea how peaceful that was."

"Oh, so you want me to put you to sleep? Is that what you're saying?"

"No."

Vicki turned off the radio and gave her vote of approval, too. "I love it when you sing, Randy. Would you play something for us?"

"How about if I play stuff we all know. Then everyone can sing." He pulled the guitar out of the case and began to strum a familiar song. He must have had his earlier conversation with Sierra in mind because the song started out,

I will trust You, Lord,
in every situation,
I will place my faith in You. . . .

Sierra sang along softly, feeling like a hypocrite. She knew only too clearly how much easier it was to sing those words than to live them.

chapter twenty

WO WEEKS AFTER THE CALIFORNIA ROAD TRIP, THE three friends met at Mama Bear's on a rainy Monday afternoon. Vicki had stopped and bought a daffodil for each of them, and the three lacy, yellow trumpets sat at the end of their long stalks in a glass of water. Sierra had already paid for the warmed-up cinnamon roll and three mugs of tea. Vicki and Sierra listened closely as Amy read from the postcard in her hand. It pictured a swaying palm tree with the word "California" arched across the top in gold letters.

> *Just wanted you to know I was thinking of you,* bella *Amy. I have thought often of what you said about how God isn't fair, since bad things happen to good people. My only thought there is that God is God. He can do whatever He wants. Apparently, one of the things He wants is to have a relationship with us. So, with a heart of love for you, I will pray that you will know God and experience this relationship.*
>
> *Ciao,*
> *Antonio*

Amy looked at Sierra and then at Vicki, her dark eyes

flashing. "Did either of you put him up to this?"

"Of course not!" Sierra said.

Amy let out a sigh and gazed into her untouched cup of tea. "You know, all of you make it hard for me to stay mad at God."

Vicki and Sierra waited for her to go on.

"You guys, all of you, keep being nice to me and caring about me. When we were at Rancho Corona, I decided I was going to hate Katie. She was your friend, Sierra, and I was sure she was going to take you away from Vicki and me. My whole life people have been taken away from me. But it was impossible to hate Katie because she acted as though she really liked all of us, not just you, Sierra. Of course, maybe it was just a show."

"It wasn't a show, Amy," Sierra said. "People really do care about you."

Amy's dark lashes blinked back the tears. "Why?"

The verses Sierra had written on Paul's valentine came to her mind, and she quoted them to Amy. "Because, 'God is love. . . . We love because he first loved us.' Love is not something that's supposed to be done on human power. It's supernatural."

"Before you start pushing me too far, Sierra, let me say this. Being with you two and Wes and Randy for five days, and being around Katie and Antonio and even Tawni, made me realize that what you guys have is very special. You really do love each other. The way you treated Warner was with a lot more kindness than I had for him."

"Did I tell you?" Vicki said, cutting into Amy's speech. "Last week Warner had to give a speech in our communications class. He talked about being a team player and looking out for the rights and feelings of others. It was a great speech.

I think the jaunt to Corvallis and the broken arm did him some good."

Sierra couldn't help but wonder if traveling all the way to Southern California would have done Warner even more good. But she was glad they didn't have to find out.

"You know," Amy said. "I think I've kind of been treating God the way Warner was treating us on the trip. He acted as if he deserved everything and got irritated when he couldn't get what he wanted. It's hard for me to admit this to you both, but I think I'm pretty spoiled and immature. I've always said it was because I was the baby of the family. But I'm graduating from high school in a few weeks. How much longer can I be the baby?"

"I was feeling exactly like that when we were at Rancho," Sierra said. "I didn't want to grow up."

"Who does?" Vicki said.

"We did, a year ago," Amy said. "I couldn't wait to have my own car and move out like my sisters did. Now I feel as though I'm not ready. My life isn't at that place yet."

"Are you saying you feel ready to turn your life over to the Lord?" Sierra asked. She knew Amy had heard all about how to become a Christian during the years she had attended Royal Academy. But knowing about God and knowing Him personally were two different things. Sierra was eager for Amy to lay down her shield and weapons and stop fighting God. In Sierra's mind, this was the perfect time for Amy to finally surrender to the Lord.

"No," Amy said firmly. "What I'm saying is that I'm taking a tiny step closer. That's all. Don't rush me."

"Okay," Sierra said, calming herself down and reaching for a piece of cinnamon roll. She knew it would be better to stuff the roll, rather than her foot, into her mouth.

"What I like," Amy said after a moment of shared silence, "is that you guys don't try to explain God to me. I mean, like this card from Antonio. He's just so honest. He says what he knows, or what he believes, and that's all. I can't stand it when people try to make excuses for God or explain why He does what He does as if they're an authority. I was just thinking yesterday that if God were easy enough to understand or to explain, then I don't think He would be big enough to run this universe or solve anyone's problems."

Vicki and Sierra exchanged expressions of amazement.

"That is so profound," Vicki said.

"Well, don't get excited," Amy said, her slight grin returning. "There aren't any more deep thoughts where that came from."

Sierra sipped her tea and then ventured to share something she hadn't told her friends yet. "I wanted to tell you guys something that happened to me on the trip. I sort of had a 'moment' with God."

"A 'moment'?" Vicki questioned with a skeptical gleam in her clear green eyes. "Where? In the chapel when you were missing that one morning?"

"No, it was at Magic Mountain." Sierra realized how ironic it was that God had seemed silent to her in the sacred chapel, but He had chosen to meet her in the middle of a crowd at an amusement park. She stored that thought away as more evidence that God's way of doing things is not the way she would choose. "I don't know if I can explain what happened. I was feeling kind of lost and by myself, and then it was as if God invisibly slipped His hand into mine and told me to hold on tight."

Amy raised an eyebrow. "You're telling us God talked to you?"

"No. I mean, yes. I mean . . . it wasn't like a voice. It was a thought. I don't know how to explain it. Have you ever had that happen to you?"

Amy looked down and sipped her tea. Vicki shook her head.

"I'm not saying I don't believe you," Vicki said. "I just never experienced anything like that."

"Well, I know it happened. I felt changed. It really felt as though God was right there beside me." Sierra knew there was no need to apologize for her experience. As Amy had said, she couldn't explain it. She didn't want to exaggerate either.

"I had a point to this," Sierra said. "But now I can't remember what it was."

"While you think of it, let me change the subject," Vicki said. "Did you send in all your papers for Rancho Corona and all the scholarship applications?"

"Yes. Did you?"

"My mom sent them off yesterday—finally. I heard my dad telling someone on the phone last night that I was going to Rancho Corona next year, as if it already had been decided. I didn't realize they were so in favor of my going. It took them long enough to read over all the information." Vicki reached for another bite of cinnamon roll, and without look-ing at Amy, she said, "Have you thought anymore about applying there, Aim?"

"No," Amy said quietly. "I don't think I want to go to a Christian college. But if I did, that's the one I'd want to go to. I can see why both of you do."

Several days after they returned from their scouting trip, Sierra had finally decided to apply at Rancho. She had dis-cussed it for long hours with her parents and even called Wes to make sure he wouldn't mind her being on the same campus. The more she prayed about it, discussed it with her parents, and accepted going away to college as the next step for her life, the more settled and at peace she felt. She realized it was time to grow up and accept the privileges as well as the responsibilities that came with the next stage of life.

Once she decided to apply, she and her parents had scrambled madly to fill out and send off all the paperwork. The finances were the biggest challenge, especially since Wes was going to Rancho and he hadn't heard back yet on any of the grants and scholarships he had applied for in their grad program. In many ways, Sierra now understood that God's will involved simply taking the next step, without knowing the final outcome, and trusting Him to lead one step at a time. Applying to Rancho had been that next step for her. She had also taken a next step with Paul.

"You both will be proud of me," Sierra said to Vicki and Amy. "I wrote to Paul last week and told him all my plans. Then, very subtly, I added, 'And how are your plans for the fall coming along?'"

"Have you heard back from him?" Amy asked.

"No, not yet."

"At least the topic is out there for you two to discuss now," Amy said, and then added, "I didn't like it last week when you said that if it was God's will for the two of you to be together, somehow Paul would mysteriously show up in your life, and it would have all been arranged without your ever talking about it."

"I agree," Vicki said. "You're the one who's always saying we have to have open communication. Even if Paul has already made totally different plans, I think it's good for him to see you're not waiting around for him. You're going forward with what you believe is God's direction for you."

Sierra smiled at her two friends. "I'm only moving ahead as far as I can see in the headlights."

"That's right," Vicki said. "You need to keep moving ahead slowly and don't try to go too fast. Keep taking it slow, and you won't get out of control."

"Or crash and burn the way I always do," Amy said.

"What would I do without all your wise advice?" Sierra said, licking the gooey white frosting from her thumb.

"Oh yeah, like we're the love experts," Vicki said. "Me and my hopeless crush on Randy. Five days with him, and he still treats me like one of the boys."

"Well, thanks to those five days, I've decided to go on a guy diet," Amy said. "I'm becoming very selective about whom I go out with. After being treated like a princess by Wes and Antonio, I realize the guys around here are junk food."

Sierra laughed. "Now, Amy, just think what a feast of great guys you would have to choose from if you came to Rancho with us."

"Oh, now *there's* a deeply spiritual reason to select a college," Amy said.

"It might not be the best reason," Vicki said, "but it's not all that bad either."

They laughed together, and Vicki said, "Can you believe we're sitting here talking about college and graduation as though it happens every day? I started thinking about it last night, and I kind of weirded out. I felt nervous about everything. I don't know why."

"You're just now feeling that way? I felt that way the whole trip," Sierra said. "That's why I went to the chapel that morning."

"And you got over the panicky feelings?" Vicki asked.

"Eventually."

"Last night I felt the same way I did at Magic Mountain when we were climbing up to the top of the Viper," Vicki said. "It was that same sickening feeling when everything is in motion and it's too late to go back."

"I know. Growing up is nothing like I thought it would be," Sierra said.

"I can't figure out how I got to this point all of a sudden, you know?" Vicki said. "I felt like I was 15 for about three years, and then I turned 16 and everything started going so fast."

"Can you believe all of us are 17 already?" Sierra said.

"I have a better one than that," Amy said solemnly. "Can you believe we're going to graduate from high school eight weeks from this Thursday?"

The gathering around the table grew silent. They spontaneously reached around the daffodils and mugs of tea and grasped each other's hands. With a wary smile, Sierra gave Amy's and Vicki's hands a squeeze.

As the raindrops roller-coasted down the front window of Mama Bear's Bakery, the three friends sat together quietly, holding on tight.

Don't Miss These Captivating Stories in
THE SIERRA JENSEN SERIES

#1 • Only You, Sierra
When her family moves to another state, Sierra dreads going to a new high school—until she meets Paul.

#2 • In Your Dreams
Just when events in Sierra's life start to look up—she even gets asked out on a date—Sierra runs into Paul.

#3 • Don't You Wish
Sierra is excited about visiting Christy Miller in California during Easter break. Unfortunately, her sister, Tawni, decides to go with her.

#4 • Close Your Eyes
Sierra experiences a sticky situation when Paul comes over for dinner and Randy shows up at the same time.

#5 • Without a Doubt
When handsome Drake reveals his interest in Sierra, life gets complicated.

#6 • With This Ring
Sierra couldn't be happier when she goes to Southern California to join Christy Miller and their friends for Doug and Tracy's wedding.

#7 • Open Your Heart
When Sierra's friend Christy Miller receives a scholarship from a university in Switzerland, she invites Sierra to go with her and Aunt Marti to visit the school.

#8 • Time Will Tell
After an exciting summer in Southern California and Switzerland, Sierra returns home to several unsettled relationships.

#9 • Now Picture This
When Sierra and Paul start corresponding, she imagines him as her boyfriend and soon begins neglecting her family and friends.

#10 • Hold on Tight
Sierra joins her brother and several friends on a road trip to Southern California to visit potential colleges.

THE CHRISTY MILLER SERIES

If you've enjoyed reading about Sierra Jensen, you'll love reading about Sierra's friend Christy Miller.

#1 • Summer Promise
Christy spends the summer at the beach with her wealthy aunt and uncle. Will she do something she'll later regret?

#2 • A Whisper and a Wish
Christy is convinced that dreams do come true when her family moves to California and the cutest guy in school shows an interest in her.

#3 • Yours Forever
Fifteen-year-old Christy does everything in her power to win Todd's attention.

#4 • Surprise Endings
Christy tries out for cheerleader, learns a classmate is out to get her, and schedules two dates for the same night.

#5 • Island Dreamer
It's an incredible tropical adventure when Christy celebrates her sixteenth birthday on Maui.

#6 • A Heart Full of Hope
A dazzling dream date, a wonderful job, a great car. And lots of freedom! Christy has it all. Or does she?

#7 • True Friends
Christy sets out with the ski club and discovers the group is thinking of doing something more than hitting the slopes.

#8 • Starry Night
Christy is torn between going to the Rose Bowl Parade with her friends or on a surprise vacation with her family.

#9 • Seventeen Wishes
Christy is off to summer camp—as a counselor for a cabin of wild fifth-grade girls.

#10 • A Time to Cherish
A surprise houseboat trip! Her senior year! Lots of friends! Life couldn't be better for Christy until . . .

#11 • Sweet Dreams
Christy's dreams become reality when Todd finally opens his heart to her. But her relationship with her best friend goes downhill fast when Katie starts dating Michael, and Christy has doubts about their relationship.

#12 • A Promise Is Forever
On a European trip with her friends, Christy finds it difficult to keep her mind off Todd. Will God bring them back together?

9803

FOCUS ON THE FAMILY®

ℒIKE THIS BOOK?

Then you'll love *Brio* magazine! Written especially for teen girls, it's packed each month with 32 pages on everything from fiction and faith to fashion, food . . . even guys! Best of all, it's all from a Christian perspective! But don't just take our word for it. Instead, see for yourself by requesting a complimentary copy.

Simply write Focus on the Family, Colorado Springs, CO 80995 (in Canada, write P.O. Box 9800, Stn. Terminal, Vancouver, B.C. V6B 4G3) and mention that you saw this offer in the back of this book. You may also call 1-800-232-6459 (in Canada, call 1-800-661-9800).

You may also visit our Web site (www.family.org) to learn more about the ministry or find out if there is a Focus on the Family office in your country.

Chances are you'll like the "Nikki Sheridan" books, too! Based on a high-school junior named Nikki, whose life is turned upside down after one night's mistake, it's a series that deals with real issues teens today face.

Have you heard about our "Classic Collection"? It's packed with drama and outstanding stories like Louisa May Alcott's *Little Women*, which features the complete text—updated for easier reading—and fascinating facts about the author. Did you know that the Alcott's home was a stop on the Underground Railroad? It's true! And every "Classic" edition packs similar information.

Call Focus on the Family at the number above, or check out your local Christian bookstore.

Focus on the Family is an organization that is dedicated to helping you and your family establish lasting, loving relationships with each other and the Lord. It's why we exist! If we can assist you or your family in any way, please feel free to contact us. We'd love to hear from you!